Booked For Murder

Maggie's Murder Mysteries, Volume 3

Morgan W. Silver

Published by Morgan W. Silver, 2021.

This is a work of fiction. Similarities to real people, places, or events are entirely coincidental.

BOOKED FOR MURDER

First edition. January 31, 2021.

Copyright © 2021 Morgan W. Silver.

Written by Morgan W. Silver.

Also by Morgan W. Silver

Maggie's Murder Mysteries
Prelude to Poison
Poised to Quill
Booked For Murder

Monday Moody
The Chrono Unit

Standalone
The Exciting Life of a Minor Character

Watch for more at www.authormw.com.

I dedicate this book to my mother.

Chapter One

It was the third week of October, and we inched closer to Halloween. We took a few special occasions quite seriously in our picturesque Cornish village of Castlefield: the Summer Festival, Halloween, and Christmas. Halloween was by far my favourite. It was the time when cold winds swept through the leaf-covered streets as people wore their knitted scarves and hurried inside to snuggle up in blankets and sip tea.

Everyone had carved pumpkins in front of their doors, and the square in front of my bookshop had orange lanterns running from my side of the street to the other side. Stanley, the baker, and his friends usually hung those up.

During the month October, he and his wife Olivia sold lovely Halloween-themed cupcakes and cakes. However, I had managed to snack on those only once a week since the month started. I was getting more and more committed to losing a few pounds. I had even looked up yoga studios in the area.

I was packing a small suitcase for my current outing while Christina—my friend and flatmate—was pacing up and down, trying to talk me out of it. She was holding my pet bunny Snowball and stroked her soft fur. We had her out of the cage most of the time when we were home. She loved doing happy bunny hops across the living room.

"I don't like it one bit, Maggie. I mean, you said it yourself—the Pembroke is cursed. People have died there. You and

Alistair almost did. And now you want to spend the weekend there?" Christina was a former beautician and now that we were nearing Halloween, she had opted for streaks of orange in her blond pixie cut, as well as dark makeup. She always managed to look both cool and beautiful.

"It will be fun," I said. "Did you not see the gorgeous invitation?" It had beautiful cursive letters and looked like it was written in the 1800s. The only downside of the invitation was that Christina wasn't going to join me; it was addressed only to me. I couldn't really blame Miles, since he had pretty much only spoken to Christina once, but whatever party he had in mind, I wish I could have brought a plus one.

Although, then I would have probably brought my best friend Eddie. He had been on multiple dates with several women—probably to erase his dating debacle from last summer; nothing is more of a mood killer than an actual killer. Nevertheless, all these dates had gone from casual promises of new dates to unanswered text messages. According to him, anyway.

Eddie needed some serious cheering up as he was spending way too much time with either me or women who clearly weren't a match for him.

Of course, I didn't know what Miles was up to, nor if it would cheer anyone up. His invitation was beautiful and mysterious, but I could only guess it was some sort of exclusive Halloween party. He was a rich lawyer, after all.

"Just be careful," Christina said. "And message me when you get there. And before you go to sleep. And when you wake up."

I laughed. "Don't worry. I'll be fine. Miles has lived at the Pembroke for about half a year now, and he's still alive."

She stuck out her bottom lip. "Just promise."

I squeezed her arm. "I promise." Then I gave Snowball a kiss on her soft head. "I can't leave you alone with this monster for too long. Before you know it, Snowball will have established complete domination."

"No, she won't. She listens to me."

"You spoil her."

"I do not."

"What did you give her the other day?"

"A plate of different kinds of fruits."

I folded my arms across my chest.

"Arranged in the shape of a bunny."

"And one in the shape of the Tardis because you said she likes *Doctor Who*." I paused. "She's a bunny."

"Fine. I'll try not to spoil her if you come back in one piece. And alive."

"There really is nothing to worry about, I assure you. Whatever Miles has planned, he's my friend, and I'm sure it will be fun."

I HAD STRAIGHTENED my auburn hair that reached my shoulders and wore a black dress with an orange cardigan to stay in theme. The invite had referred to the dress code as casual, but I still wanted to look stylish. I wore a long grey coat and wheeled along my small but heavy suitcase. The Pembroke was a brief walking distance and technically I could always dash home and get something, but I wasn't sure what Miles had planned. I only knew it would last all weekend, so naturally, I had overpacked.

I had left through the back of my bookshop, The Wicked Bookworm, which was my flat entrance, and made it past my aunt's occult shop and across the small bridge.

My aunt was spending time with her boyfriend Gus, who was doing quite well for someone who was terminally ill. They'd had a lot of film nights in the past few days and Nancy had cooked for him almost every night.

The sky was grey, and it was beginning to get dark. As I made my way towards the small hill on which the former hotel stood, something red and small flashed in the corner of my eye. I stopped.

Oh, no.

Since I was in the editing phase of my latest Detective Black novel, I had been locked up in my office for a while now and had the pleasure of not running into evil poultry, but I guess Pandora must have smelt my innocence.

I hurried along as fast as I could without running. There was no need for such desperate measures yet. Nothing popped out to attack me, and with relief, I could spot the majestic Pembroke estate. It was a Victorian mansion with ivy climbing alongside the building. It had large windows and Miles had done his best to put his own stamp on it. He had created a lovely rose garden and added a few benches and bushes to make it less bare. And inside, he had transformed it from hotel to home. I was actually looking forward to—

Pandora stood still several feet in front of me.

I abruptly came to a halt and held my breath for a moment. Only two people had the skill to defy Pandora, and neither of them were here. There was a time where I thought we'd reached an understanding—right after she helped me attack a murderer. Apparently, that understanding was over.

"Hi, Pandora. How are you? I like what you've done with your feathers," I said in a squeaky voice.

The red chicken cocked her head and stared at me.

Maybe I could throw my suitcase at her.

She let out a loud screech—her battle cry—and I was forced to run. I went around the nearest car and into the cobbled street. Dragging my suitcase behind me was not easy on these cobbles, but it did protect me from an assault. We ran the entire way to the Pembroke where her interest was diverted to a teenager who was walking his Boston Terrier. He had headphones on and was staring at his screen. Rookie mistake. The streets of Castlefield were not safe as long as Pandora was around.

Oh, well. Every man for himself. I continued on to the double doors of the former hotel. Behind me sounded another one of Pandora's screeches and a lot of barking.

I rang the doorbell and glanced over my shoulder. I'm sure they would be fine.

Both doors opened and a man in his forties with salt-and-pepper hair stood in front of me in one of those *Downtown Abbey* suits. He looked like a fancy butler.

"Welcome to the Pembroke," the man said in a mellifluous voice and bowed. "Your invitation, please?"

"How interesting." Detective Black popped up without warning, as he usually did, and surveyed the butler. "Maybe Miles is into some role playing?" He wiggled his dark eyebrows at me.

I swallowed and fished my invitation out of my coat pocket. If Miles had told everyone to come in costume except me, I'd kill him. I handed the man my invitation.

"Excellent. Welcome, Miss Matthews. I am Warren, the butler this weekend. May I take your coat and suitcase?"

I surveyed four suitcases behind Warren. One was bright pink.

"Err, sure. Thank you, Warren." I shrugged off my coat and scarf and handed them to him after he had closed the double doors.

He put my stuff in a coat closet to the left while I observed the newly decorated hall. The staircase was now painted white and the carpet was gone. It had broad, dark wooden steps that were a nice contrast to the light banister. The floor in the hall was white marble and the reception area had been taken out. I had been here a few weeks ago for drinks with Alistair and Miles, so I knew there was a large room to the left with a bar, sofas, and a fireplace at the end of the room. The room to the right was long and had large windows that brightened the place.

It had two entrances, one leading to the entrance hall and one leading further down the corridor, behind the staircase. It had been transformed into a nice, modern area and had a fireplace and sofas, while in the back there was a large dining room table. Miles had recently put a piano in between those two areas.

Warren led me into the living room/dining room, though I knew Miles spent most of his time in his office upstairs. He even had a TV there.

Several people were sitting on the sofas in front of the burning fireplace. My eyes immediately went to Alistair with his dark hair and sharp eyes. His lips curved into a charming smile as soon as he noticed me. I returned the smile and felt my cheeks warm. Eddie's unruly red hair caught my attention next.

"Eddie?" I had no idea he and Miles even knew each other's names.

He grinned sheepishly. "Hey, Mags. Before you ask, I have no idea what's going on."

Opposite them were two other people—a man and woman in their mid-forties.

"Rest assured. Your host will introduce himself shortly and explain the rules for this weekend," Warren said from behind me.

"Oh, God. This isn't some weird sex party, is it?" Eddie asked with a horrified expression.

"Of course not," we all said simultaneously.

He held up his hands.

"No," Warren added. "This is a murder mystery weekend."

A MOMENT LATER, WE were all at the long dining room table. The couple had introduced themselves as Geoff and Brenda. The man had dark blond hair and was wearing an expensive blazer while his wife had chestnut curls and wore a dress with a very low v-neck. They looked a bit snooty, and I wondered if they were Miles's friends.

The table was set for one more person, seated next to Brenda. We were just chatting about everyone's occupations—Geoff was an accountant and Brenda a librarian—when Warren walked in again. I was just about to discuss books with Brenda and was curious to learn if she knew my Detective Black mysteries, so I was a bit disappointed.

Warren cleared his throat. "I would like to introduce your host for this weekend: Miles Mortimer." He stepped aside and Miles strode in.

He was dressed in a sharp suit, the kind of suits he wore when he was in a courtroom, and gave a blinding smile. Every time I saw him, it struck me how handsome he was. It also made me wonder why he was still single. He came from a wealthy family—and a dip shit of a dad—but he had still worked hard and become a successful criminal lawyer. I could imagine he was used to having things a certain way and perhaps a woman didn't quite fit. She would have to be able to keep him on his toes.

We had spent some time together, sometimes just us, sometimes with Alistair, but in the past few weeks I hadn't seen much of either men due to my editing schedule.

"And it was totally worth it," Detective Black whispered in my ear.

I still had some final editing to do, but I couldn't say no to what I thought was a Halloween party. Now that I knew it was a murder mystery weekend, I was even more excited. I had always wanted to do one of these things.

I wondered if Alistair would get the role of detective, since he actually was one.

"Welcome, everyone. You've been invited to my hopefully annual murder mystery weekend. There is one more guest set to arrive, but he informed me he is running late. In a minute, Warren will hand out cards with information about who you're going to be in the next few days. The front contains details you'll share with each other so you know who's who and so we don't have to introduce ourselves the next morning. The information on the back is stuff you can't share with everyone. Until this bell rings—" Miles glanced at Warren, who was now suddenly holding a bell. He rang it. "—you are not to break out of your role. A murder will be committed, and you are to act according to your character at all times. Some things will be scripted, some improvised. So be sure to read your cards carefully. I am the only one who will not have a role. I'll simply be Miles, the host. Any questions?"

"When is dinner? I'm starving," Eddie said.

Miles grinned. "It is ready and will be served in mere seconds."

"Thank goodness. Don't suppose there's any chance it will be fish and chips? I am really in the mood for that." Eddie looked at Miles hopefully.

The corner of his mouth twitched. "No," he said curtly. "I'm afraid not."

I sniggered. Miles was a great cook, and I doubted he would consider fish and chips worthy of a murder mystery weekend dinner.

Miles left and Warren started handing out envelopes with our names on it.

"Take a look," Detective Black said.

My hands were burning to rip the envelope open; everyone else was doing the same.

"Was this your idea?" Alistair asked, while he opened his envelope.

"I wish. Does this mean you didn't know about this either?" I asked.

Alistair shook his head.

At the top of my card was a name in beautiful letters. "Okay," I said out loud. "I'm Estelle Waverly. A model. And my boyfriend is Nathaniel." I glanced around.

Alistair shifted in his seat. "That's me." He blushed as he looked at me.

Of course it is.

Detective Black was chuckling in the corner.

Alistair cleared his throat and studied the card. "And I'm an art dealer."

Geoff and Brenda were called Alan and Moira. They were married and both on holiday from America. Moira was supposed to be a teacher and Alan a car salesman.

Eddie's character was Richie, and he was related to Miles. That was all.

"Great, that means I'm totally going to die. It's not fair. I just came here for food. How am I going to eat when I'm dead?" Eddie pushed out his bottom lip.

"You do realise you won't really be dead?" I chuckled.

"When I commit, I commit," he said. "But I'd like to formally complain that it's not fair to kill off the only red-head."

"If you do turn out to be the victim, it's not because of the colour of your hair," I said.

He narrowed his eyes. "What is that supposed to mean?"

"Well, I'm excited already," Brenda said. "This is going to be fun."

We all agreed. Then I turned to Eddie. "Since when are you friends with Miles?" I whispered.

"I saw him and Alistair at the pub once. We started chatting. We've been playing an online game together for a while."

"You have?" I said way too loud. I really had no idea, and I couldn't picture Alistair or Miles playing video games.

Just then, Warren wheeled in a cart with several bowls of potato soup. He placed them on the table along with Miles. Miles gave me a wink when he reached me.

"You're blushing." Detective Black now stood to the side and shook his head at me. "I hope your character can keep her reactions in check. Oh, now you'll finally know what it's like to be one."

I chuckled.

"What?" Alistair asked.

"Nothing."

Eddie slurped loudly as he downed the rest of his bowl.

"You're done already?" Brenda asked, her eyes wide.

"That's nothing," I said, waving a hand. "He once ate a large pizza in three minutes."

Her eyes widened even more.

Geoff chuckled. "That's quite the feat, young man."

"What?" Eddie looked up from his bowl. He glanced around at us. "What?"

I couldn't help but laugh.

Detective Black sighed. "Yep. He'll definitely be the murder victim."

Chapter Two

The doorbell rang.

Soon, a man in his late thirties entered the room. He had blond hair and light-blue eyes. He didn't appear as posh as the others, in his jeans and shirt.

"Ah, so it is a dinner party. The invite was very vague. I'm so sorry I'm late. I'm David." His accent told me he was from Manchester.

This was my chance.

"No, it's not a dinner party. You've been booked for murder," I said dramatically.

Everyone was quiet, and the man just blinked at me.

"See, this was once a hotel." I beamed at him. "No? Nothing? Okay, fine. It's a—"

"Welcome," Miles said, as he appeared in the open doorway. "To the murder mys—"

"Mystery weekend!" I quickly finished for him.

Alistair chuckled next to me but quickly transformed it into a cough.

Miles explained the weekend again and Warren handed David his card while he took the bottle of wine from him. When Miles headed back to the kitchen, I followed him.

"A murder mystery weekend without consulting me, huh?" I asked.

He turned around and flashed me a grin. "It's way more fun when it's a surprise."

I folded my arms across my chest.

"Oh, is that why you had your little outburst? Because you wanted to be a part of this?"

"I—I did not have an outburst. I was just excited, that's all. I'm a mystery author. Why did you not consult me? I could have helped."

"Because I wanted you to experience it. Besides, I managed just fine without you."

"I can plan it and experience it at the same time. I'm a great multi-tasker. Once, I knitted a scarf while taking a bath."

The corners of his mouth pulled upwards. "Knitting naked. How daring of you."

"Tell you what, I shower naked too."

He gasped. "Oh, no. I must tell everyone."

We grinned at each other.

"Okay, promise me I can help next year."

"Whatever makes you happy, dear. Now, please return to your seat and promise me you'll enjoy yourself this weekend."

"I will. Thank you. This was a really cool idea." I hugged him.

His breath tickled my ear as he let out a short laugh, and his perfume smelt enticing. "I knew you would love it. It's about to get better, though."

"I'm sure it will. And why didn't you tell me you and Eddie were gaming buddies?" I asked.

"I thought you already knew." He shrugged. "He made me buy a Playstation. Who knew those things were fun? And Eddie is surprisingly talented at killing people."

"Something we have in common. I just use a pen, not a game controller."

"Basically, we are all very dangerous. It's a wonder we're allowed outside."

"With Eddie's eating habits, it really is." Not that I was one to talk. I could be equally bad. Of course, I wasn't going to admit that to Mr Perfect. "Okay, I'll see you back in there. I look forward to the murder."

"I can see why you were a murder suspect the first time we met," he said dryly.

I stuck out my tongue.

The others were all engaged in conversation. David was chatting with Alistair about his latest hike, while Eddie and the married couple were discussing vintage cars. Later, Alistair informed me that David's character was a professor of archaeology named Dan. Over the course of the dinner, we managed to keep the conversation light and general. Miles had not joined us; he had been busy serving us the food together with Warren.

After we had finished a delicious chocolate dessert, he returned to conclude the evening.

"You are free to enjoy my home and do as you wish, but remember that tomorrow you are someone else and must react accordingly at all times," he said. He had a glint in his eyes and was clearly enjoying his role.

We applauded—not sure why—and then everyone else went up to their rooms, including Eddie. He was hoping there would be a jacuzzi in his bathroom.

Miles returned to the kitchen, so that left Alistair and me.

"Finally, a non-lethal murder in this place. It was about time," Alistair said. "Still, it's weird to have this murder mystery weekend here, of all places."

Detective Black smirked at me. "Don't worry. When you get scared, you can snuggle up to Alistair."

I ignored him.

"Yes, it's almost like nearly dying is traumatic and our aversion to this place is natural," I said.

His lips quivered. "Are you mocking me?

"Not at all. It's just that thinking about nearly dying is making me sarcastic."

"We could just leave, you know. We don't have to stay here." Alistair's expression turned serious.

"No, we can't do that to Miles. He put a lot of effort into this weekend. Besides, this is not the same place as it was back then. Miles has put his stamp on it, and this place is no longer filled with death traps. Also, this will be a good way to think of murder as something fun." I frowned. "That came out wrong, but you know what I mean."

"Yes. This will be about the most fun thing about mysteries: solving them."

"Exactly. Speaking of which, did you know the three others are all actors?" I grinned at him, proud of my deduction.

"What? What makes you think that?"

"Ha. He didn't even realise. Go on, show off," Detective Black said.

"David is from Woolfield," I said.

Alistair narrowed his eyes for a moment. "Ha, that's easy. You must have seen the pictures he showed of his hike."

"Yep. But Brenda and Geoff are also from Woolfield."

He tapped his finger against his lips as he contemplated how I could know that. Then he shook his head in defeat. "How do you know that?"

"Their suitcases in the hallway. They had mud on the wheels, and in the coat closet was a wet umbrella. It rained for a brief while about thirty minutes before the time I arrived, which means they had walked in the rain. That indicates they didn't come by car, but by bus. The train station is too far, and Brenda wore high heels, so it has to be the bus."

"That still doesn't explain they came from Woolfield. It means they were on the bus about fifteen to twenty minutes, which means they could have only come from Greenfield or Woolfield."

I held up my finger. "Yes, but I overheard Geoff mention roadworks, and those are currently taking place on the long road between the Castlefield Forest and Woolfield. Also, I saw a fallen bus ticket by the pink suitcase."

He chuckled. "Okay, impressive. But, how do you make the leap to them all being actors?"

"Because they were all vague about where they were from, which means they didn't want us to know. Also, if they all know Miles and are from the same village, it's unlikely they're strangers to each other, yet they act as if they are. The most logical conclusion is that they're all actors. Warren too, probably."

Alistair's eyes darted across my face. "You're really something," he said softly.

I felt my cheeks get warm and looked away. "No, I'm not."

He touched my chin and forced me to look back at him. "You are."

"For crying out loud," Detective Black said, "If you don't kiss him, I will."

My heart beat wildly against my chest. It was so tempting. Just as I was gathering my courage, Alistair cleared his throat and turned away.

"I'll go check out my room and get settled. I'll see you around." He then rushed out of the room without so much as a final glance at me.

I felt my heart sink into my shoes. Why was he acting so weird? Thank goodness I hadn't actually kissed him.

Miles told me to have fun, and that was exactly what I was going to do. I deserved to relax, not fret about a certain detective. I studied the card again. There were secrets on the back that I was supposed to spill over the course of the weekend, and there was a fight I was supposed to be having with Alistair about a supposed affair.

Miles had really done his best to make this as fun and realistic as possible.

Maybe he should try writing a novel.

"Miss?"

I jumped and whirled around.

Warren gave me an apologetic smile. "I'm sorry. I didn't mean to startle you."

"It's okay," I said.

"Would you like to go see your room?" he asked.

"Sure. It better have a jacuzzi," I muttered.

IT TURNED OUT THE BATH did, in fact, have jacuzzi jets. It had also been completely redone, though I doubted Miles had done that with every bathroom; it would have cost too much. Either way, I was grateful. Now it looked nothing like the bathroom I had found my first dead body in.

I was eager to dive in and try out the jacuzzi jets, but first I phoned Christina. She picked up on the second ring.

"Hey, you," I said.

"Hey. You're still alive. That's a good sign."

"Well, someone is about to die real soon," I said.

"What?!"

I couldn't help but laugh. "Sorry, let me explain." I informed her of everything that happened so far—except for the fact that I had wanted to kiss Alistair. She was still his ex, and the main reason I had planned on keeping my distance. It was my own fault. Just because he looked so kissable didn't mean I should kiss him.

"A moment of weakness," Detective Black said, having popped up again. "I have them all the time. Mostly when it comes to beer. I always get one pint too many and end up serenading the lamp post outside my house."

I made a zipping motion across my lips while Christina responded to my recap.

"You're a model, huh? And who is your boyfriend going to be?"

Right. Might as well tell the truth. "Err, Alistair."

"Miles is playing cupid," Detective Black said and made the shape of a heart with his hands.

She let out a giggle. "Alistair is Miles's friend. That doesn't surprise me."

I wasn't sure what to say to that.

"What's wrong? I told you to go for it."

"Yes, you did. I just—oh, there's someone at my door. I gotta go. I'll call you later." Before she could say anything else, I hung up the phone.

"Coward," Detective Black said.

"I don't know what you mean."

"You say you don't want to be with Alistair because of Christina, but really you're just scared."

"I am not scared of anything. I laugh in the face of danger."

There was a knock on my door.

I shrieked.

"You were saying?" Detective Black said.

"Just go back in my head." I moved to answer the door.

"Good, you're here," Eddie said and darted in to plop himself onto my bed with a sigh.

"What are you doing?"

"I'm hanging out with you." He was wearing jeans and a black shirt, like usual. He never wore anything else. Not even while I was wearing two layers under this dress.

I also had the sneaking suspicion he didn't want to be alone. He'd spent a lot of time with me, and while I was editing, he'd apparently been gaming with Alistair and Miles. I liked that new development. Mainly because Eddie's only other friend was Brian, and in my opinion he could branch out.

"Did you know Miles was planning this?" I asked.

"No. I'm not sure I would have come if I did."

"Why not?" I sat down on the bed next to him.

"Murder mysteries are kind of your thing, Maggie."

"Okay, but this will be fun. You'll see."

He sighed. "I guess."

I don't know what came over me, but all these months of sulking were not like Eddie, and something snapped.

I grabbed his ear.

"Ouch, what are you doing? This is what my granny did when I stole too many biscuits from the jar."

"You need to stop wallowing. So what if the last girl you really liked turned out to have some issues? Stuff happens. You just get back in the saddle. You've been dating other women, right? It's just a matter of time until you come across one you really like and who likes you."

Eddie freed his ear from my grasp with a shake of his head. "That's not it."

I frowned. "What do you mean? You've not been yourself these past few months. You've been spending a lot of time with me, and you've been serial dating."

Eddie gave me a look.

"Oh, oh," Detective Black said. "He's done something."

"Eddie," I said in a stern voice. "What have you done?"

He grabbed my hand. "I felt bad, not because I had been duped. Okay, not *just* because I had been duped. Mostly, it was because I got you into trouble. If I had realised what was going on, you wouldn't have nearly died last summer."

I gasped. "It wasn't your fault. And I had no idea you felt this way."

"And I haven't been going on dates."

My eyes widened. "What have you been doing then?"

"I've been taking self-defence classes. If you are ever in trouble again, I can protect you."

Tears blurred my vision. "Oh, Eddie." I hugged him.

When I pulled back again, he brushed away my tears.

"Is this why you installed those cameras in the bookshop and above the stairs to my flat?"

He nodded as a blush spread out across his freckled cheeks. "Yeah. Actually, Alistair advised me on what kind of camera to get. And I think I inspired Miles to pick up boxing."

I raised an eyebrow. "Really?"

"He said that in this homicidal village, he'd probably get to use those skills."

We looked at each other.

"Pandora," we said simultaneously and then laughed.

"Although, to be fair, I think Pandora would actually win any boxing match. She's too good."

"The other day she attacked a group of cyclists. One of them nearly rode his bike into Harold."

"Yikes." I made a face. In his wheelchair, the vicar wasn't the quickest to get out the way. They were lucky an actual collision hadn't occurred.

"Speaking of evil chickens, how is your dating life?" he asked. "Don't think I haven't noticed the googly eyes at DS Ashworth."

I chose to ignore that statement. "The last date I had was with the guy Harold had set me up with."

"That was months ago!"

"Okay, calm down. I didn't realise I had a quota to fulfil."

"You do. At least four dates a month," he said with a smirk.

I had actually joined a dating app, but didn't want to mention it just yet. It was very likely it wouldn't lead to anything.

"I'm going to check out the library," I said.

"Oh, do you want me to—"

"No." I held up my hand. "Look, I appreciate your concern over my near death experiences in the past year, but you're not my guard. I can handle myself just fine, and the next murder that will occur will be fake, so..." I gave him a kiss on the cheek. "Be free."

He gave me a sceptical look. "I'm your best friend, I'll always worry."

"I get that, but you're not responsible for my safety."

"Fine. Just, no more murders. Okay?" He was practically begging with his eyes.

"Only fictional ones," I said.

Chapter Three

The library was also Miles's study. I had helped make that happen when I made sure all the books belonging to the previous owners were relocated. I'd even found a couple of old books that I had sent to an old friend who worked in the antiquarian book trade. Now, the space was filled with two large bookcases on both walls on either side of the entrance, and there was a large mahogany desk and a fireplace. Two armchairs were placed in front of the fire, and there was a globe bar where Miles stored all his whisky.

The fire was burning, and Miles was in one of the armchairs, his back to me.

"Penny for your thoughts," I said.

He looked up and smiled. "Just enjoying the quiet before the storm."

"This is the first time you're having this many people over, right?" I took my seat in the armchair opposite him.

He nodded. "Yes. So far, my favourite part has been the cooking. Drink?"

"Why not?" I said. "And have you ever considered doing anything with your love for cooking?"

He poured me a whisky with lots of ice and handed it to me, then sat back down. "You mean job-wise?"

"Yes."

"Oh, no. I could never do it as a job. That would make it stressful. As a hobby, it relaxes me and makes me happy. I'd rather keep it that way. Besides, I like the job I already have."

I took a sip of my whisky. It was nice and smooth. "Why did you want to do this murder mystery weekend? I mean, you clearly won't use this as a hotel, so what then? It's so big for just you."

"I want to use it for events. Murder mystery weekends, weddings, parties, anything, really. Once a month, no more."

I frowned. "That surprises me." The fire crackled next to us and the warmth radiating from it spread through my legs. I could easily stay here a while. Being surrounded by books helped, of course.

"I used to live in a big house with my parents, but it always felt empty. We had two maids and a nanny for me, but I was always the happiest when I had a birthday party or when I had friends over. The flat I had before was nice and big, but it somehow highlighted how alone I was. At least here, I have the opportunity to fill it with laughter." He chuckled to himself. "It sounds stupid when I say it out loud."

"It's not stupid at all. And I think it's a great idea. Castlefield is a cosy village where people love getting together. This will still give the Pembroke a purpose, and it's too beautiful not to be used to its full potential."

"Agreed," he held out his glass and we clinked.

I took a sip and stared at him. "You've made Alistair my boyfriend, huh?"

He grinned. "It's just a matter of time."

AFTER TWO DRINKS WITH Miles, I returned to my room. I figured I would read in bed and mentally prepare for being someone else tomorrow. In one night I'd go from a book-shop owner/author to a model with Alistair as my boyfriend. Ha. Miles really was something.

As I arrived at the door, a young woman headed my way. I hadn't seen her earlier.

"Hi," I said.

She had long, dark-blond hair and thin eyebrows. She didn't look particularly friendly, but maybe that was because of the smirk on her face.

"Hey."

"I didn't see you at dinner," I said, curiosity taking over.

She stopped and looked me up and down. "I'm one of the maids during this weekend."

"Maid?" I asked and tried not to stare at her long, fake nails. Those didn't seem useful for that kind of job. Or any.

"Yeah. Have fun these next few days." Her grin widened. "I know I will."

She walked off with wiggling hips.

I narrowed my eyes at her.

"What an odd thing to say," Detective Black said.

"I know."

"What do you know?" Alistair's breath tickled my ear.

I nearly hit the ceiling. I turned around with my hand over my fast-beating heart. "To what do I owe this heart attack?"

He winced. "Sorry, it was just too tempting not to sneak up on you."

"I'll keep that in mind."

He must have taken a shower because his hair was still damp. I breathed in the scent of his aftershave. At least he wasn't wearing his usual suit but had changed into dark trousers and a cream-coloured jumper.

"I'm going to hang out with Miles and Eddie for a bit. Want to join us? I promise we'll keep the gaming talk to a minimum." His lips pulled into a smile.

"No, don't worry. You guys have fun. I'm going to read in bed for a while and then sleep. I'm sure we have quite the weekend ahead of us."

"I think so too. Miles went through a lot of effort."

"I bet. If only he'd asked for my help. I could have made things easier for him."

Alistair's smile only widened. "I think he wanted you to have something to solve without risking your life."

"He did?"

"Yes. Last summer was both impressive and worrisome. I mean, I know it all ended well and you unmasked a murderer, but it could have gone either way. And that's a scary thought."

I bit my lip. Alistair had told me about his partner who died during an arrest, and it also explained how overly attentive he'd been that summer. It made me feel fuzzy and warm knowing I had friends who cared so much for me. To be fair, I'd be equally concerned if the roles had been reversed. In a way, I was glad it had happened to me and not them.

It only cost me a few therapy sessions.

Alistair touched a strand of my hair. "I'm not saying that to make you feel bad. It wasn't your fault."

"It also wasn't yours."

His lips pulled down for a brief instant. "Thanks."

I hugged him and rested my chin on his shoulder. "I mean it. It wasn't."

He wrapped his arms around me. "Thank you."

"You know, it's great that you're friends," Detective Black started, "but have you considered becoming friends with benefits?" He flashed a cheeky grin.

I pressed my lips together to keep from laughing and let go of Alistair. "Have fun with the boys. I'll see you tomorrow."

"Sleep well."

I entered my room and took a bath. Afterwards I even put on a facial mask and felt properly pampered. I changed into snugly pyjamas before settling in the large double bed with my e-reader. I just had to remember not to touch my face or I'd get this clay-like substance on my fingers.

I also went to the window by the bed to close the curtains. In the garden I made out two figures and it took me a moment to figure out who they were.

David and the woman who is supposed to be the maid.

"Clue?" Detective Black asked.

"I don't know."

I closed the curtains and hopped into bed. I'd read about four chapters before I started nodding off. Which meant I had to get this clay off my face and put my e-reader away. It wouldn't be the first time falling asleep while half-reading.

I got up to go to the bathroom when a knock sounded on my door.

"Murderer, potential lover, or ghost?" Detective Black said from behind me.

I opened the door, despite the fact that I looked weird right now. I instantly regretted that as Alistair stood before me.

"Ah, potential lover it is," Detective Black said dryly to my right.

Alistair had his arm against the door post and the look in his eyes wasn't as sharp as usual.

"You're drunk," I blurted out.

He held up his finger. "Tipsy, my fair lady. There is a difference." He staggered into the room, and I had to hold him in order to prevent him from falling. "Okay, never mind," he said. "Maybe I am drunk."

"You think?" I closed the door. It was best if I gave him some water to sober up, and once I had washed my face, I could escort him to his room.

He let me guide him to the bed where I sat him down as he observed my face. "Is it me or is your face more beautiful than ever?"

I snort-laughed, then clasped my hand in front of my mouth, and then cringed as I realised I now had clay all over my hand.

Detective Black was laughing.

"Just stay here while I wash my face and contemplate killing off my lead character."

This shut Detective Black up.

"I love—" Alistair's voice trailed off as he mumbled.

I whirled around instantly and strode back. "What? What did you say?"

He had let himself fall back on the bed and snored.

Damn it.

I contemplated waking him, but he looked so adorable when he was asleep. Although the snoring wasn't cute at all. I hurried back to the bathroom and washed my face. At least my skin was nice and smooth now.

When I returned to the bed, Alistair was no longer snoring, but he still had his eyes closed and didn't move. I nudged him twice, but he didn't stir. Would it be okay to let him sleep here for the night? I nudged him again and leaned closer to him. "Alistair," I whispered.

He turned half-around, opened his eyes briefly, then groaned.

"Are you awake?" I whispered again. "Do you want to stay here? You can, if you want to."

With his eyes closed, he reached out one hand and slipped it in my hair. He brought my face closer to his and as my heart bounced around in my chest, his lips touched mine. It was a soft and drowsy kiss, and his delicious aftershave was intoxicating.

When he let me go and his head fell back on the bed, his eyes were closed. There was a dreamy smile on his face, though.

I held up my hands and let out a soundless scream, then put my hands over my mouth.

"If you start throwing confetti around, I'm going to smack you," Detective Black said, but he was smiling too.

I couldn't be entirely sure how awake and/or drunk he had been, but it counted. If only it could have lasted longer.

He was still draped half across the bed, so I first positioned him so that his head was on the pillow. It was quite the struggle, since Alistair kept trying to roll away from me.

And here I thought we'd had a moment.

I finally managed to get him in the right position without waking him, which was when I moved on to his shoes. For some reason, they refused to come off, even though I'd untied the shoe laces. I got on the end of the bed, half on top of his legs as I wiggled off his right shoe with great difficulty.

Alistair suddenly let out a loud snore and jerked his leg, causing me to jump and fall off the bed.

I stared at the ceiling with my hair half over my face and blew it away. Then I gasped and triumphantly held up the shoe.

Victory.

After I showed the other shoe who was boss, I draped my robe over the completely oblivious drunk detective and lied down next to him, under the covers. I kept the light next to my bed on so I could stare at him until I fell asleep.

Chapter Four

A knock woke me up the next morning.

"Wake up, Miss Waverly. Breakfast is ready," Warren's voice said from the other side of the door.

Waverly?

"Yes, your character," Detective Black said.

Right. I sat up straight. "I'll be there soon," I shouted back.

There was something I had to remember.

Alistair.

The right side of the bed was empty. Had I imagined it? Was it a dream?

I checked my phone. A message from Alistair.

Thanks for putting up with this idiot, it said.

I smiled and texted back: *You're never an idiot.* Then I jumped out of bed and got ready for the day. This weekend was going to be special. I could feel it.

When I got downstairs, everyone but Eddie was already there. Even Miles, looking quite like a lord in his lovely suit, was at the head of the breakfast table, reading a newspaper. There was a sparkle in his eyes. He was enjoying this already.

My eyes zeroed in on Alistair who was at the buffet table. I remembered I was supposed to be someone else, so I didn't smile at Miles or Eddie but went straight for a cup of tea. Alistair joined me within seconds.

"Thanks for letting me crash in your room last night. I just need to check something."

"What?"

"I know this may sound silly, but I had a dream." He looked up at me and blushed. "I dreamt that we kissed. I mean, that was a dream, right?"

I studied his worried face. It looked as if he wanted it to be a dream. Did he?

"Y—yes, it was."

When I saw the relief on his face, I added: "I think I would have remembered if I was kissed."

"Yeah, no good. I mean, that would have been stupid. Can you imagine?" He chuckled.

"Haha, yes, so stupid."

He returned to the table, as I blinked away a few tears. I don't know why I was so upset over it. We had agreed to stay friends. Heck, it had been my decision. Mostly. Anyway, I was fine. I was totally fine.

I put my tea next to Alistair's seat and grabbed a plate. I stuffed it with fried eggs, three pieces of toast, two croissants, and a cinnamon roll.

"Hello," Brenda started in an American accent as I sat down opposite her. "You're wearing a lovely dress," she said to me.

I took three huge bites out of my cinnamon roll.

"Thanks. I'm a model," I said with a full mouth.

Everyone at the table glanced from my stuffed face to my stuffed plate.

"What?" I said as I glared at them all.

"Nothing," they all said simultaneously.

We all talked about general pleasantries. There was no drama yet. It seemed we were just going to enjoy a normal breakfast.

I wondered who the victim would be.

"I slept like a log," Brenda said. I had to hand it to her, I would totally buy that she was American. She stretched. "I'm so glad we're on this holiday. England is so beautiful."

"It's just a country," Geoff said with a shrug.

"Well, you would say that, wouldn't you."

Okay, I was wrong. Drama was about to happen.

Yay.

Brenda turned to us. "All he ever does is work. It's a miracle I got him to come on this vacation. It's a wonder he even remembers my name."

I expected Geoff to go off at her, but instead he pushed back his chair, regarded Brenda coolly and walked off.

Brenda rolled her eyes. "Such a drama queen, that man."

I nearly laughed but managed to hold it in. I wanted to say something, but had to remember I was someone else now.

"Aren't we all, darling," I said with a smirk.

Alistair raised his eyebrows at me. I winked at him.

To my surprise, he blushed.

"This weekend is going to be so much fun," Detective Black said from behind me.

Eddie strolled in. He had his jeans lower than usual and was wearing a hat the other way around. He also walked with swagger. Not something I wished to see so early in the morning.

"He looks like he's got a badger in his trousers," Detective Black said.

"Wassup, innit," he said in a cockney accent.

"Oh, boy," Alistair muttered under his breath.

"Ah, yes," Miles said and rose to his feet. "I haven't introduced you to my cousin Richie. He's from London."

"Word," Eddie said.

I bit my lip to keep from laughing.

"I dunno what you was rabbiting about, innit, but I'd like to take this moment to tell these ladies that they got lovely minces. You get me?" He pointed to his own eyes and then to mine.

"Thank you so much, Richie," Brenda said. "At least someone's noticed."

"I still don't get what minces are," Alistair whispered.

"I'm pretty sure he's referring to our eyes," I whispered back.

"And how long do you think he studied cockney rhyming slang?" He took a sip of coffee.

"Hours and hours." I grinned. It surprised me how well Eddie was pulling this off. Yes, he was going overboard, but I hadn't expected that and it was nice to see him enjoy himself.

He sat down and got some bacon and eggs with a cup of tea. "Say, cuz. Can I borrow some bees?" He lowered his voice but was loud enough for us all to hear.

"I bet this is another clue," Detective Black said. "But why would he need bees? For honey?"

Miles raised an eyebrow. "Bees?"

The contrast between Miles's posh demeanour and Eddie's casual one made me hide my smile behind my cup of tea. Miles had really done a good job creating these characters.

"Money, innit? I just need it to start my new garage, so I can become a mechanic. I had a lot of bees saved, but it got stolen. Would you Adam and Eve it?"

If bees meant money because it rhymed with honey, then Adam and Eve would mean believe. Ha, I was getting the hang of this.

"No, I do not believe it, and no, I will not give you any more money. We have discussed this."

Hmm. Miles had said he'd just be the host, but that didn't mean he wasn't involved in the mystery. Clearly, this was part of the weekend.

"Come on, mate, we don't have to have a bull about it. We is family, innit?"

My inner grammar critic sputtered at that.

"The discussion is over. My decision is final," Miles said.

"We'll see about that." He got up. "Alligator." Then stormed off.

Brenda chuckled nervously. Something that suited her character. "Your cousin seems lovely."

Miles gave a polite nod and returned to reading his newspaper.

After breakfast, I wanted to check out what Miles had done with the garden. It was also a beautiful day with the sun peeking out from behind a stack of clouds.

"Nathaniel, darling. Care for a stroll in the garden?" I gave him a sultry smile. Or at least, I tried. I wasn't sure how to do it. It could be that he thought I was holding in a burp.

"Sure, I'd love to, honey." We went to the coat closet to retrieve our coats and my scarf. Eleanor, the vicar's wife, had knitted it for me and it was a beautiful burgundy colour with white stripes.

We went out through the front entrance and walked around the house. Alistair held out his arm so I could loop mine through his.

"I hope you don't have a hangover," I said, and felt a stab as I remembered the kiss and realised I'd be the only one.

"No, I just felt groggy this morning. I drank a lot of water and had a cool shower before I came down. That helped. I hope I didn't make too much of an ass out of myself last night. To be honest, I don't remember much. Had you done something to your face?"

I smiled. "Yeah, I had a facial mask on. And don't worry, you did nothing wrong. You slept like a baby. A snoring baby."

He chuckled. "I always snore when I have something to drink. I hope I wasn't too loud."

"Don't worry about it. So, how does it feel to be my boyfriend?" I looked up at him.

Alistair's expression changed and I followed his gaze. By one of the rose bushes stood the young woman I'd run into the day before. The one who said she was the maid, but I suspected she was an actress as well.

"You are probably right," Detective Black said from beside me. "No maid would actually wear that."

She had on a typical sexy maid costume. The cheap ones you find around Halloween. What was her name again?

"Oh, hello," she said as she spotted us. She was twirling around a rose she had just plucked and only made eye contact with Alistair. She wore her long dark-blond hair down and swayed her hips as she approached us. Well, Alistair. I was as invisible as a ninja during a blackout, apparently.

"I'm Valerie," she said and smiled seductively as she handed him the rose.

He didn't take it, though. His jaw tensed. "No, thank you. Keep it." His tone was even.

Wow.

She narrowed her eyes and for the first time she glanced in my direction. Then she smiled at him again and tucked the flower in his breast pocket.

"I'll see you around." She then winked at him.

If I had been a cat, my tail would have been twitching. Although, technically, I could still pounce and scratch her eyes out.

As soon as she disappeared around the back of the mansion, I grabbed the rose and threw it over my shoulder.

"You would think she would have been freezing," Alistair said, shaking his head.

"So you didn't think she looked hot?" I folded my arms across my chest.

He laughed. "No. Why? Did it look like I thought that?"

"No. But she's—I mean, I wouldn't blame you if—"

"Estelle," he said, levelling me with a stern gaze. "You know you're the only one for me." He put his arms around me and kissed my forehead.

I mumbled incoherently. I could get used to this.

Chapter Five

"Why do I get the feeling this Valerie is going to be trouble?" Detective Black said while I wrinkled my nose.

I wasn't sure why, but I got the impression that she hadn't been playing a role.

We continued walking past the side of the mansion and towards the back. There was a stretch of grass and near the bottom of the hill, the woods began. There was a bench close to the patio and we sat down.

There was a chill in the air, but it wasn't exactly cold. Still, I was glad I had on a long coat that protected me from the cold of the iron bench.

"So, Estelle," Alistair began. "Remind me again how we met." A cheeky grin spread across his face.

There had been no info about that on my character card so I could use my good old imagination.

Alright, where would a model have met an art dealer?

The corner of my mouth pulled upwards and I turned to him. "Don't you remember? We met at a doggie fashion show. Pretty Pooches, it was called."

Alistair's eyes widened. "A what now?"

"Yeah, I remember it like it was yesterday. You had brought your toy poodle Snickerdoodle who had been styled by a very famous dog styler. I was in the audience and we met afterwards." I put my hand on his arm. "I'm still so terribly sorry about Snickerdoodle and that terrible washing machine accident."

Alistair bit his lip. "Yeah, she never saw it coming."

"Anyway, we got to talking about Snickerdoodle's ballerina outfit and it was love at first sight."

"Yeah, that's right. And now we live a nice, wealthy life."

"Oh, definitely. We eat diamonds for breakfast."

"Ouch," Alistair chuckled.

We let silence descend between us as crows cawed in the distance. The sky was cloudy and it smelt like cinnamon. Probably because Miles had some sort of pie in the oven for tea time.

"I love the sound of crows," Alistair said.

"Me too."

"Me three," Detective Black whispered. He was sitting on my other side but disappeared when I glared at him.

"You know, I once got lost in these woods," Alistair said as he pointed to the treeline at the bottom of the hill.

"You did? How old were you?"

"I was like seven or eight. I was with a few of my friends and we were looking for adventure because we were bored. It was around this time of year."

"I imagine an abandoned, cursed mansion was a good place to look for adventure, especially around Halloween."

"Exactly. We had crept into the mansion which was dusty and messy, and our plan was to look for ghosts. I believe we had just watched the film *Ghostbusters*."

I raised my eyebrows. "You are more similar to Eddie than I realised."Although, since the Welsh ghost hunters had left us last spring, Eddie and his friend Brian hadn't brought up their love for anything ghostly.

"Don't worry, I don't believe in ghosts anymore."

"So I'm guessing a ghost didn't chase you off into the woods then?" I pictured a sheet with two holes chasing a young Alistair down the hill.

"No. My friends decided to mess with me—why me, I don't know—and started disappearing one by one while we explored the ground floor. Only one of us had a torch and that was me. Even so, I couldn't find them and got scared. It was so quiet I could only hear my own breathing. I thought a monster or ghost had taken them."

It was difficult to imagine the always poised and cool Alistair to be afraid of anything. What amazed me even more was that he was telling me about it. He was actually opening up to me more and more.

"Anyway, I panicked when I started to hear strange noises and I bolted out of the mansion and just kept on running."

"Into the woods," I said softly.

"Into the woods."

"And then what happened?" I shivered and it wasn't from the cold.

"I got lost. I was lost for about three hours, and it was getting dark."

I swallowed. "I'm sorry. You must have been so scared."

"Yes, I was. But at some point I came across a tree with some crows in it. They started to circle above me."

I grabbed his sleeve. "Why? Did they attack you?" Crows wouldn't do that, would they?

He chuckled. "No, they started flying in the same direction, making sure I was in sight the whole time and led me back to the village."

My mouth dropped open. "You're kidding."

"Nope."

"No wonder you have such a way with Pandora. Apparently you have a special bond with winged creatures."

Alistair smiled. "It's a gift."

"It certainly is. I'm glad you made it out okay. Sorry about your rotten friends."

"Don't worry. They were terrified when they couldn't find me. They had told their parents who were just about to look for me when I showed up. They got into a lot of trouble, but I was just relieved to be back. I didn't blame them. They were kids. Intention matters and they hadn't intended for that to happen."

"I suppose that's true." In his line of work that mattered a lot. I guess it mattered in any type of situation.

I cleared my throat. "My mother has a mental illness. When I was young, she was convinced of conspiracies and threats everywhere."

Out of the corner of my eye I saw Alistair go very still. I had never mentioned my mother, though he knew a bit about her, as did everyone in this village. Still, I never discussed her, not even with Nancy. Not unless she brought her up.

Even Christina didn't really know much. I had simply told her my parents weren't in the picture and that my aunt was like a mother to me.

"When I was six, somewhere around November or December when it was freezing, my mother had become convinced that the government had replaced me with a clone that was spying on her. She drove me to the edge of a forest that was about an hour away from home and dropped me off, then left."

Alistair looked at me, but I couldn't quite make eye contact.

"She eventually told my father when he came home and noticed I wasn't there, but I had been there for hours and had to go to hospital because I had blue lips and couldn't stop shivering. I was also dehydrated."

Alistair scooted closer to me and put his arm around me. "Is that when you moved in with Nancy?"

"Yeah. Not straight away, but pretty much."

"I'm so sorry," he whispered as his voice sounded shaky.

"It's okay. I survived." I tried to sound brave but the tremor in my voice gave me away.

Alistair squeezed my shoulder. "Thank you for telling me."

"Sure. Just don't tell anyone else."

"I promise." He smiled at me. "And the same goes about my story. I can't have people knowing about my secret super power."

"Right. Your nemeses might take advantage."

"Exactly."

We sat like that for a while until it got cold and we were getting curious about the next clues regarding the fake murder.

"Maybe it will be another fight," Alistair said as we hung up our coats in the entrance hall.

"Or maybe it will be stolen glances between two characters who shouldn't be stealing glances."

"Or spilled blood." Alistair raised an eyebrow.

"I must say, I've never found a murder to be this fun."

Detective Black appeared. "I am so insulted."

"I'm going to find Miles. See you later." He gave me a kiss on the cheek.

I blushed. "See you soon." I watched him go past the staircase and disappear and was about to go to my room when I heard a noise coming from Miles's office.

I opened the door and peered inside.

Eddie was struggling with a large painting of a cottage covered in snow.

"Eddie!" I said without thinking.

He looked up. "It's Richie, innit. Quickly, close the door."

I did as he said. "Right. Sorry, Richie. I am not very good with names." I remembered something from my character card. Richie was going to ask me something and I would have to say yes.

"Richie is stealing a painting from his cousin," Detective Black said. "At least, that's what my guess is. It must be because he needs money."

"What are you doing?" I asked.

"I'm taking this painting. My cuz owns me. I'm just gonna have to ask you to keep it on the down-low. You feel me?"

"What's in it for me?"

His eyes darted from left to right.

I wasn't sure if I was supposed to ask that, but I couldn't imagine Estelle agreeing to it so readily.

"What do you want?"

I shrugged and pretended to think. There was something Estelle really wanted. "I want you to convince Nathaniel to propose to me. I've been dropping hints left and right and he still hasn't done it. You talk to him, man to...well, man." I narrowed my eyes at him.

Ha, I was quite good at pretending to be arrogant. I could tell from the spark in Eddie's eyes that he was enjoying this.

"Done. Though I don't see why anybody wouldn't propose to such a fine specimen as yourself, innit."

At this I couldn't help but laugh.

Eddie grinned.

"I'll see you around, Richie." I gave a small wave.

As soon as I shut the door behind me, there was a loud crash coming from the kitchen.

"Another clue," Detective Black said. "Things are certainly exciting at the Pembroke."

"As long as no real bodies show up, I'm all for it," I muttered.

Chapter Six

Around tea time we gathered in the sitting room by the fireplace. Warren had brought in the cake Miles had made on a cart, along with a large tea pot and delicate tea cups.

I wondered briefly if I had to decline the cake since I was supposed to be a model, but then realised that was silly. One never says no to cake.

Just as Warren was about to step into the corridor, he ran into Valerie. She was wearing a different maid outfit and I wondered if she had been told off about the earlier one. I exchanged a glance with Alistair.

"Ah, there you are," Warren said tightly.

"I just came to tell you all the beds have been made and I've cleaned the kitchen," Valerie said in a friendly tone. She sounded and seemed very different from the Valerie we bumped into in the garden.

I guess it proved that she had been more herself then.

"Excellent."

"Well, 'ello, gorgeous," Eddie said as he sprang to his feet and approached them.

Valerie giggled.

"Maybe we should take a stroll later," Eddie said.

It was weird to see him flirt with such bravado whereas he usually went bright red. Especially when talking to someone as attractive as Valerie.

"Maybe," she said with a coy smile, quite different from the way she had looked at Alistair.

Warren cleared his throat. "Please get back to work, Valerie." He glared at Eddie and then followed Valerie out of sight.

Eddie shrugged and sauntered back to the armchair he had been sitting in to continue his cake and tea.

"I love tea time," Brenda said. "I wish Americans took a moment to have some tea and something to nibble on."

Geoff scoffed. "Why don't you move here then?"

Brenda narrowed her eyes at him.

"Do you smell that?" Detective Black said as he sniffed the air next to me. "I smell a fake divorce."

Alistair shifted his weight and leaned towards Miles. "You know, I've spotted some beautiful paintings that I could take off your hands for a lot of money."

Miles gave a small smile. "No, thank you. I am not interested in selling any of my heirlooms. They are invaluable to me."

Eddie and I looked at each other.

"Yep, Eddie is going to die," Detective Black said with a chuckle.

We continued our tea time while pretending to get to know each other. Alistair asked Brenda and Geoff about their supposed lives in America while we talked about how we had met and what my life as a model entailed.

I enjoyed telling them about the fashion shows and parties with celebrities and it felt nice to be someone else for a moment. Miles had come up with a great form of entertainment. The women of the Castlefield Book Club would have loved this as well. In fact, if he was going to make this a regular event, they would probably attend every single time.

Especially if there was going to be cake.

Miles stood up after we had finished our cake and tea. "I've set up a fun game of cricket outside and invite you all to join. Grab your coats and follow me."

Noises of excitement filled the air as everyone donned their coats and followed Alistair through the corridor and kitchen to go outside.

Miles stopped halfway across the large kitchen as Valerie and Warren stood by the kitchen counters. Valerie was in tears.

"I'm afraid I'm going to have to let you go and that decision is final," Warren said with a placid expression.

"B—but why?" Valerie sobbed.

"I told you. You are not performing well enough."

She cried even louder as she buried her head in her hands.

"Ah," he said as he noticed us. "I'm so sorry you all have to see this."

"Oh, poor girl," Brenda said with her hand to her heart.

"Mate, she's too hot to sack." Eddie shook his head.

"Good help is so hard to find," I added in my most snobbiest tone.

Valerie ran off past us, her cheeks red. She was very good at crying on cue. I could never do that.

Warren adjusted his white gloves and gave a bow of the head, then also left the kitchen.

"Well. I should take care of that. Why don't you all make it outside and get the game started," Miles said and ushered us through the French doors and onto the patio.

He disappeared with a smile and left us to play a game I had never played.

Surprisingly, Geoff and Alistair knew how to play and they taught us as we went along. It was more fun than I would have thought.

Eddie was a natural and occasionally pretended his bat was a sword while Brenda laughed and Alistair shook his head.

Miles returned after about ten minutes and joined the game.

I had now officially changed my mind about who the victim would be and was looking forward to things moving along.

This would be the most relaxed I'd ever be while solving a murder.

THINGS WERE QUIET LEADING up to dinner time, so I phoned Christina. It was weird to think that I could just walk out of this mansion and be with her in ten minutes, but I enjoyed the feeling of being in this different world with different characters.

I updated her on everything that had happened so far. She laughed so hard she was crying when I told her about Eddie's role.

"How's Snowball doing?"

"She's fine. Don't worry, I'm not spoiling her too much. I did have to move your knitting basket, because she started to nibble on it."

"I'll have a word with her when I get home."

Christina sniggered. "As long as you're having fun, that's all that matters. I'm sorry I was so worried earlier."

"Don't apologise for something like that. You meant well. Besides, you're not the only one who is a worrier." I told her about Eddie's boxing and the cameras that had been installed because of the last murder I'd tried to solve.

"Yeah. I know. Eddie told me about the boxing. Then when the new cameras were being hung up, I put one and one together."

"And here I thought we were just being modern. Eddie told me that all shops had them and really didn't want to be left behind. I can't believe I didn't realise it."

"That's because you're not scared yourself. It's not like it wasn't a big deal for you, but you bounced back and refuse to live in fear. I admire that about you."

"Well, the person who hurt me was put away. I can't treat everyone I meet like a potential murderer."

"True. And don't worry, Eddie will get over it too. He just needs some more time and to deal with it in his own way."

"I know. And as weird as it may seem, I think this weekend is actually helping all of us. Miles really did an amazing job at making murder fun. And I feel like it's all bringing us together. I hope there will be more murder mysteries that more of us can join."

"Yeah, I'd like that as well. It really does sound interesting," Christina said.

"Be careful. You might become a fan of murder as well."

"Not like you, but I do understand the need to uncover a mystery. It's like solving a puzzle, isn't it?"

"Definitely. And it's so satisfying when everything clicks." It was kind of addictive.

"Well, I'll leave you to your clicking then. Don't forget to bond with your boyfriend."

"Ha ha."

"See you."

"Later," I said. "Give Snowball a cuddle from me."

"Will do."

I hung up and let myself fall onto the double bed. Fear was a funny thing. It was used as a warning, that something is wrong. But fear could also be used to stay inside someone's comfort zone. And comfort zones could remain very small that way.

I was afraid of plenty of things. Maybe murderers could not hold me back, but there were plenty of things that did.

Telling Alistair about my mother reminded me of how I had experienced a lot of abandonment, not just with my mother. Only Nancy had been a comfortable constant. My anchor. It was entirely possible that Alistair was the final thing I could not stand to lose and so I preferred not to even try.

"You think?" Detective Black said as he rolled his eyes. "Do you want an applause for figuring that out?"

"Shut up or I'll write a Pandora into your next book."

Detective Black shuddered.

"Thought so."

I got a text message from Miles that it was time for dinner and so I freshened up and put on a purple dress before going downstairs.

As I opened the door to leave, Alistair was about to knock.

"Oh, hi," I said.

"Hello, Estelle. You look lovely." He held out his arm.

"Thank you, Nathaniel." I took it.

"I wonder what will be on the menu," Alistair said.

"Murder," Detective Black said from behind me.

"Me too." I ran a hand through my hair which I had straightened. I figured if I were to be a model, I'd put in a tiny bit more effort than usual.

I twisted my ankle and if I hadn't been holding on to Alistair, I would have fallen.

Heels also qualified as putting in more effort. Unfortunately.

"Are you okay?"

"Yeah, I'm not used to—I mean, I slipped." I was supposed to be used to high heels.

Alistair grinned. "Do you need a piggy-back ride?"

I nudged him in his side and he laughed.

Just as we made it halfway down the stairs, there was a scream followed by shouting. Alistair and I froze and looked at each other.

Then we took two quick steps before I lost my balance again. Alistair grabbed me by the waist so I wouldn't tumble down the stairs, then, in the interest of time, he lifted me in his arms and hurried down the stairs with surprising speed. He put me down at the bottom of the staircase as we went into the living room.

Valerie was by the fireplace. A poker by her head. There was a pool of blood around it as she stared at the ceiling.

Chapter Seven

I had seen my fair share of dead bodies—well, only two, but it was two too many—to know that she wasn't really dead, but it was pretty close to being realistic. They had really done their best with the fake blood and pale skin. It probably also explained the smug smile that Miles failed to hide behind his hand.

"She's dead, she's dead," Brenda yelled hysterically.

Alistair and I shared a glance of relief. Just like me, he clearly had experienced a moment of panic at the scream.

"What happened?" Alistair asked while I started fanning myself, pretending to be shocked.

"It seems," Miles said, "that Valerie, the maid, has been murdered by one of us."

"And how do you figure that, Sherlock?" Eddie asked.

"Nobody else entered this building. The doorbell didn't ring and I have cameras by the front and back entrances that record when there's movement. They haven't recorded anything since a few hours ago and this clearly recently happened. The blood hasn't dried."

"How terrible to think it was someone here." I clutched Alistair's arm for good measure.

We all jumped as Warren hit a gong. It was the sign that we could break character.

"There is a bowl I put up on the mantelpiece with index cards and a pen. Any time you think you know who the killer is, write the time and date and the name. You can only guess twice. Your last card counts. You can win a prize if you've got it right. Questions?"

Nobody said anything and Warren hit the gong again.

"I guess I'll go and call the detective," Miles said and fished his phone out of his pocket.

Alistair and I looked up.

"Detective? Who is the detective?" I asked.

Miles just smirked and walked off.

"A new character," I said. "How exciting. I wonder who it is."

THE DOORBELL RANG AND a moment later, the platinum blond beehive that was my aunt's hair caught my attention first. It was the only recognisable part of her. Her usual black or purple flowy outfits had been exchanged for a grey suit. Her brightly coloured lips were a natural colour and she had an unlit cigarillo dangling between them.

Even Alistair's jaw had dropped.

I looked at Miles over my shoulder and smiled at him. He gave an imperceptible nod in return.

If anyone deserved a break from normal life at the moment, it was her.

"Well, well, well, what have we here?" she said as she eyed us all.

"I'm afraid someone has been murdered," Warren said. He was standing closest to Nancy as he'd just let her in.

"I can see that. I may have one glass eye, but the other one works just fine."

Warren actually blushed at that.

I bit my lip to keep from smiling. Smiling at a pretend murder scene would not look good and pretend prison would be awful. Think of all the pretend non-scones.

"Now, you would all save me loads of time if you'd just tell me you did it." She took out the cigarillo and twirled it around. "I'm waiting."

We all looked around the room at each other in awkward silence.

Eddie cleared his throat. "Listen, lady, I don't think that's how it works, innit. Clearly the murderer is bonkers to kill off such a lovely young bird."

"First of all, it's lady detective, young man," Nancy said, stepping closer to Eddie. "And second of all, I know more than anyone how it works. I've been a detective for so long I've mostly forgotten everything there is to know about it."

This elicited a chuckle from the supposedly deceased Valerie.

"So why don't you keep your lips zipped until I ask you a question." She glared at Eddie for good measure.

He shrugged and threw himself onto the sofa, lifting his foot on the coffee table.

Nancy knocked it off in passing and checked out Valerie's body.

"It looks like she was hit in the head by that poker there. That means she really pissed someone off. I need all your names and anything you can tell me about the victim. But first," she said, pausing for a moment, "we need the crime scene unit."

Judging by the astonished look on Miles's face, this was not part of the plan and it didn't surprise me in the least. Nancy was a wild card.

"Warren, was it? If you so please," she said with a grin as she stuck the cigarillo back into her mouth.

He went back into the corridor and after the sound of the front door closing with a bang, the Castlefield Book Club poured into the room looking like marshmallows. They were dressed in the same white protective outfits that actual CSU members wear, and they had on blue gloves, though some of them had on those yellow rubber cleaning gloves, and what looked like plastic sandwich bags around their shoes.

All of them were present. Olivia who was usually at the bakery, helping out Stanley, looked particularly cheerful, but that probably had something to do with the fact that she pretty much always smiled. Eleanor, the vicar's wife, winked at me. Ava stood there with a tool box and I wasn't sure if I wanted to know what was in it. She craned her neck to get a look at Valerie. She was probably checking to see if she could spot her chest rising and falling. She was also one of those people who would always look for inconsistencies and 'mistakes' in films and then loudly point them out.

Jessica and Phoebe had their arms linked. They were neighbours and friends, though they could also fight like crazy. Jessica was short and round and Phoebe was long and thin. They had a bucket with what looked like cleaning supplies. I guessed they were fans of props.

Lily narrowed her gaze at each and everyone of us, as if she was suspicious. She had in her hand a contraption that was a cross between a hoover and a toaster and I imagined it was one of her own inventions. Who knew what it could do? Probably not what it was supposed to do, as with most of her inventions.

Poppy was the oldest of them all, being eighty-three, and she had her gaze fixed firmly on the coffee table and the empty plates. It was as if the intensity of her gaze could magically summon new pieces of cake.

"Alright, ladies. Let's get started. I want the works. Fingerprints, DNA, and...other evidence." Nancy cleared her throat. "You guys all move to the dining table, where I'll question you all." She grabbed a notebook from the inside of her jacket and clicked a pen.

Nancy followed us to the end of the long room and had her back to the living room area. "Alright, let's all take turns stating your names, where you were at the time of the murder and what your relationship was with the victim. Tell me everything because I will know when you're lying." She glared at Eddie. "Looking at you, Red."

He gasped. "How rude, innit."

We all did as she had asked. I was in my room, Nathaniel was in the study, Miles was in his office downstairs, Moira was taking a bath while her husband Alan was exploring the mansion, and Dan and Richie were in the garden as Warren was taking care of things in the kitchen.

I thought back to seeing Valerie and David in the garden. Of course, Warren had just fired Valerie, so that was a huge clue.

Warren confessed to that straight away, while David and the others maintained that they didn't really know Valerie. That she was just the maid for the weekend. Alistair and I had to confess the same thing. This brought the focus back on Warren.

"And why had you fired her on the spot?" Nancy asked. "You say it was because she didn't do her job well enough. But it couldn't have been so bad that you had to fire her straight away. You only had one more day to go."

"Well, no. It was pretty bad."

"Why?"

"What?" Warren asked.

"Why was it bad? Name an example of what she did that was so inadequate."

"Err, well, I can't think of anything right now." He looked down at his hands.

"Aha. That's because that wasn't the real reason, was it? Admit it," Nancy said as she slammed her fist on the dining room table, making most of us flinch.

"Look, it's none of your business," he said through clenched teeth.

"Murder is my business." Nancy jutted out her chin. "That poor girl is lying there dead, and—"

A loud giggle sounded from the other side of the room.

Nancy slowly turned around to observe Poppy and Lily using makeup brushes to 'dust' the victim's face and arms. Valerie had refrained from moving, but couldn't stop herself from giggling.

"Ladies!" Nancy yelled.

"Sorry, but you said you wanted the works," Lily yelled back from across the large space.

Nancy snapped her head back in the direction of Warren. "Talk."

He pushed his chair back. "I fired her due to personal reasons and they're none of your business. Now, unless you want to arrest me for firing her, I'm going up to my room."

Nancy let out a frustrated growl that signalled to Warren that he had won this battle. With a satisfied grin, he left the room.

"As for all of you, don't go far. I'm not done just yet. I will inform you all about what the CSU are working hard to discover."

I glanced behind Nancy.

Poppy had fallen asleep while Phoebe and Jessica fought over a torch and Lily was still 'dusting' Valerie. Eleanor was pretending to take pictures and Olivia and Ava were talking in a corner.

"Dismissed," she said in a clipped voice.

ALISTAIR AND I WENT back to my room, laughing. We weren't supposed to break out of our roles, but when we were together, it was impossible not to.

Besides, the twist with the book club ladies was too funny.

"You know, I think they should really make a career switch and join the CSU. Think of all the crimes they could help solve." I closed the door behind me while Alistair sat down on the bed.

"Are you kidding? They'll probably end up assaulting all the dead bodies."

"Second death by tickling." I chuckled. "Valerie handled herself pretty well."

"Yes, perhaps she can be professional after all."

I sat down next to Alistair. "Any thoughts yet as to who the killer could be?" I wiggled my eyebrows.

He tilted his head. "Right now, suspect number one is Warren."

"Agreed. We know too little to add anyone else to the list. I also don't see how Richie's money problems or the American tourists fighting has anything to do with Valerie's death. The poker suggests it was something that happened in the heat of the moment while they were standing in front of the fireplace."

Alistair ran a hand through his hair. "Wow, I can't believe we're actually trying to solve a fake murder. I've never done that before."

"I have. All the time." I glanced at Detective Black who winked back at me.

"And you do a very good job."

I felt heat flare across my cheeks. "Thank you. Coming from you, that's high praise. You are a very good detective."

"I appreciate you saying that. It's not an easy profession."

"Yes, it must be very difficult sometimes. Have you ever failed to solve a murder?"

"No, but I have to admit that I'm like a dog with a bone. I just can't back down. I'm not sure if that's a good thing."

"I think it is. And I'm sure the families of the victim think the same thing," I said.

He nodded and smiled at me.

At that exact moment we both received a text message from Miles, asking us to come down again.

"Show time," I said.

Chapter Eight

We were all sitting at the dining room table again. The book club ladies had disappeared, much to my chagrin. I had been looking forward to more of their shenanigans.

Nancy was pacing up and down.

"Someone has died, but we are getting closer to finding out who the killer was," Nancy said. "It may not be enough to bring that poor girl back from the dead, but—"

"Hiya," Valerie said cheerfully as she entered the room. "Do we have any ice cream? I'm famished." The attitude from earlier had apparently returned.

Geoff turned red and looked around the table with a panicked expression.

"Valerie," he hissed. "You're supposed to be dead."

"I know," she said with a sly grin. "If any of you want to know what it's like to make out with a ghost, now is your chance."

Geoff pushed back his chair and turned to Nancy.

"Excuse me, Detective. I need to use the restroom." He darted past Valerie and grabbed her arm to drag her along.

She let out a shriek of discontent but had no choice but to follow him into the corridor.

During this entire time, Nancy had remained calm. She really was committed to this character. Kudos.

We all turned our attention back to her and she gave us all a poised smile.

"We found fingerprints on the murder weapon," she said ominously.

We all stilled.

There was a tingle that travelled up my spine. This was actually getting exciting.

"The fingerprints belong to Moira."

Our gazes were pulled to Brenda who started fanning herself.

"Oh, dear," she said. "Well, I did use the poker when the fire was burning last night."

"And you have no reason to dislike or harm the maid?" Nancy asked.

"Of course not. I don't even know her."

"That ain't true, innit," Eddie said. "I saw them talking near my room and then leave when they realised I was watching them."

"Is that so?" Nancy asked. "Does it have anything to do with the fact that you gave up your first child for adoption? A girl who would have the same age as Valerie?"

Brenda's bottom lip started trembling. Wow. She was a good actress.

Geoff had picked the right moment to return to the room.

"What?" he asked as he approached the table. "You gave up a child for adoption?"

"It was b—before your time," she sobbed.

"And Valerie was this child?" I blurted out.

"Indeed," Nancy said.

Detective Black popped up next to Nancy. "And the plot thickens."

After this minor plot twist, we had dinner. Miles had cooked a simple spaghetti, but it was delicious. Geoff and Brenda didn't join us and I wasn't sure if it had anything to do with Valerie popping up earlier. I do know that Geoff was very angry.

David stayed behind with us, though, and entertained us with a story about a drunk tour guide in Greece. I wasn't sure if it was something he'd made up as his character or something that had really happened, but he sure knew how to tell a story.

So far, David's character Dan hadn't done anything suspicious, unless the meeting with Valerie in the garden was part of the weekend. Either way, it made him the most suspicious.

After dinner, Eddie and Alistair joined me for a game of cards in the living room. The fireplace was burning and the poker that was supposed to be the murder weapon was still missing. Nancy had left before dinner and would probably be back tomorrow again with another revelation. I couldn't wait.

"Hey. There is already a card in the bowl." Alistair pointed to the bowl on top of the mantelpiece.

"That's way too early," Eddie said in his normal accent. "Who do you think added a card already?"

"I did," I said.

"What?"

"You did?" They said simultaneously.

"How could you possibly know already?" Alistair asked.

I shrugged. "Intuition. But I could be wrong. I've got two tries, remember?"

"Still. Who do you think it is?" Eddie leaned forward, his eyes big.

"I'm not telling. You have to guess yourself. It won't be fun otherwise." I winked at him.

Eddie and Alistair exchanged a look.

"What?" I asked.

"I think I know what you're going to ask for every one of your birthdays from now on," Eddie said with a sigh.

"I'm having a normal amount of fun, okay? You guys are having a blast too." I pointed at them accusingly.

"True," Alistair said. "But you're having an extra amount of fun. It's probably because this is so similar to you writing a mystery. Except that now you're one of the characters."

That was kind of what it was like.

I shrugged. "I don't see why you're complaining. At least in this case no vicious killers can come after me."

Eddie and Alistair exchanged another glance.

"Or are you planning on installing cameras here too? And sticking to my side in case you need to box someone off me?"

Alistair cleared his throat while Eddie just glared at me.

"We did that because we care," Eddie said.

"I know. I'm just saying, don't complain about me enjoying a fake murder."

"We're not. We're teasing you. There's a difference." Eddie stuck out his tongue.

"I love you too." I stuck out my tongue as well.

"Gin!" Alistair calls out.

"Gin? I thought we were playing Texas hold 'em?" I frowned.

"We are. I was just messing with you."

Eddie smiled at me. "Look who is becoming a wild card."

I giggled.

"I see. Now we are teasing me."

"Don't you feel special?" I asked and checked my hand again.

"So special."

We continued playing for a few hours. Eddie went up to his room first. Then we went as well. Alistair walked me to my room.

"I can't believe tomorrow is the last day already," I said as I leaned against my doorpost.

"Yes, it went by fast."

"Indeed." Somehow I didn't quite know what to say. I wanted to say something. Something...more. But the words were lodged somewhere in the back of my throat, refusing to come out.

"Well," Alistair said. "I guess I should be going."

"Yeah." Again I was searching for words, unable to find them.

"Bye."

I sighed as I watched him go. "Bye," I said softly.

I STRETCHED AND CHECKED my alarm, not feeling rested in the slightest. It was midnight. Why had I woken up? I was dreaming of something warm and fluffy.

"Snowball?" Detective Black asked. "Or Alistair?" He chuckled.

"Shut up," I mumbled and realised my mouth was dry. Perhaps a steaming mug of tea would help put me to sleep.

I put on a robe and my slippers and opened the door. There was one light on at the end and one at the start of the corridor. They helped me find my way to the staircase and down I went. I took out my phone to use the torch. I hurried through the corridor and all the way to the back where the kitchen was.

The entire place was nice and quiet and I was proud to realise I wasn't afraid in the slightest. Whatever curse I believed to be in place once, it had now been lifted. This was Miles's home now and it felt like it. A warm, safe place. Perhaps a bit too big to feel properly cosy, but it was getting there.

I put the kettle on and secured my robe even more tightly, feeling a sudden chill. Were the French doors open? I held out my phone as I walked over. One of the doors was ajar. I opened it and peered into the darkness. I couldn't see a thing.

"Were those voices?" Detective Black said from behind me.

I strained my ears. I thought I could make out a woman and a man talking, but the increasing loudness of the kettle made me close the door and hurry back to the counter. Whatever they were doing, it was none of my business. It could not have been part of the murder mystery weekend because nobody could have anticipated me getting out of bed and going down to the kitchen.

What if it was Alistair with that Valerie?

It was as if a hand made of ice grabbed my heart. No, no. I was being silly. Besides, even if it was them, it would be none of my concern.

"And yet you'd be concerned," Detective Black said with a raised eyebrow. It made him look smug.

Great, I was never going to sleep. I poured myself some white tea and hurried up to my room. I wanted to try and forget I had overheard anyone and go back to my warm and comfortable bed.

I ended up reading to take my mind off things, then having to pee because of the tea, and finally fell asleep around two in the morning.

By the time Warren knocked on my door to announce breakfast, I was moody.

I dragged myself out of bed, washed up and packed the few items I had taken out of my suitcase since Friday. That way I wouldn't have to pack tonight.

Everyone was already downstairs when I arrived. I scooped up some scrambled eggs and grabbed two slices of toast before sitting down between Eddie and Alistair.

I eyed Alistair as he took a sip of his coffee.

"Sleep well?" I asked him.

He nodded. "Yeah, I did. Did you?"

"Peachy." I took a bite out of the toast. "You went to bed after you dropped me off at my room?"

He looked up at me with a question mark in his eyes. "Yeah. Why?"

"No reason." I took another bite. "And you didn't leave after that?"

He frowned. "No. Again, why?"

"No reason."

He opened his mouth to say something, but decided against it and continued his breakfast while occasionally glancing at me.

"Estelle, darling," he said after most of us had finished breakfast. "Want to go for a stroll in the gardens?"

I shrugged. "Okay." Perhaps a little fresh air would lift my spirits.

We went to get our coats. Since I couldn't find my scarf, Alistair lent me his. I wrapped it tightly around my neck, then realised it smelt like him and loosened it. I really had to do something about this crush.

"Ha," Detective Black said. "As if it's just a crush."

"Shut up," I said.

"What?" Alistair asked.

"What?" I said.

He narrowed his eyes at me. "Are you okay?" We made our way outside and strolled past the side of the mansion towards the back again, just like we had the morning before.

"Yeah, I just didn't sleep that well."

"Why not?"

"Don't know. I fell asleep, but then I woke up. Not sure why." Perhaps I had a lot on my mind.

Alistair cleared his throat. "I was wondering, are you still in touch with your mother?" he asked.

I turned my head to him. He had his gaze fixed ahead of us.

"She's tried calling me a few times. According to my aunt, she's going to be released from the institution she's at soon."

"And your father?"

"He's got a new family. He sends me birthday cards but I always throw them away."

"I'm sorry," he said and reached out to grab my hand.

If he hadn't done that, I would have fallen flat on my face when I tripped over something. Instead, he caught me and we both turned to look at what I'd tripped over.

Nausea rippled through me.

"Oh, no," I said. "That's Valerie."

"Yes." Alistair's voice was tight. "And she's definitely dead for real this time."

Chapter Nine

By the time Alistair was on the phone with his colleagues, I was pale and trembling. Detective Black's comments telling me to breathe didn't help one bit. It wasn't just because I had literally stumbled on a dead body, it was the fact that she had been strangled with my scarf.

At least, that's what it looked like. She had bloodshot eyes, and the scarf was wound tightly around her neck. There were also scratch marks on her neck, as if she had tried to claw at the scarf and free herself.

Why would she be wearing my scarf? Or had the killer been wearing it? Either way, it was entirely possible that I would never wear a scarf again.

Alistair had to stay with the body, which meant that I had the unfortunate task of telling the others.

The only luck was that they were all still at the breakfast table, though Geoff and Brenda had just gotten up and were about to leave.

"Excuse me," I said in a voice that was too high-pitched.

Miles got up. "What's wrong? You look very pale."

"I'm sorry to have to tell you all this, but Valerie is dead."

"We know that," David said.

"What do you mean?" Miles asked.

"She's been murdered outside. Alistair is calling it in as we speak and guarding the crime scene. I'm supposed to tell you

all and keep you in the same room until he can question us all."
I swallowed, my tongue feeling like sandpaper.

"She's really dead?" Miles asked. He inhaled sharply.
"H—how did she die?"

"We'll have to wait for the coroner, but it looks like she was strangled."

David got up to his feet. "You're lying. This is part of a joke, right? You're lying."

"No, I'm afraid not. I'm sorry."

"Does Alistair need any help?" Warren asked, a defeated look on his face. "Can we do anything?"

"I don't think so," I said.

"Are you okay?" Eddie asked as he got up and put his arm around me.

"I feel a bit shaky."

"Come on, sit down." He helped me to the chair closest to me.

Miles squeezed my shoulder and then also sat down.

"Perhaps we should clear the table. I don't think I can stand looking at this food," Brenda said in her normal accent.

"No. Nobody leaves this room." I sounded more bossy than I had intended.

"Why not?" Brenda asked, sounding a little offended.

"Because you're all suspects."

There was a moment of silence as everyone took that in.

"Oh," she said meekly and sat down.

ALISTAIR AND HIS PARTNER DC Daniels—Hugh—approached us an hour later, though it felt like an eternity.

Alistair had his detective face on, meaning he looked like nothing could shake him. He'd had that same serious expression the first time he questioned me about a murder, also in this room, though in the back.

The Pembroke was cursed.

"I'm DS Alistair Ashworth, and this is my colleague DC Daniels. I realise this is a big shock to everyone, including me, but I'm afraid there's been an actual murder. Valerie Cooke was killed in the garden last night."

Brenda gasped dramatically, despite the fact that we already knew this, and the others started firing questions at Alistair.

Eddie just squeezed my shoulder. His jaw was set.

I had promised him no more murders. I'd even found the body. Again. He must have been convinced I was going to start poking around. And he'd be right.

She'd been strangled with my scarf.

Alistair held up his hand. "I understand that you are all in shock and that you have many questions, but right now, I'm the one asking questions. Someone killed her and it's my job to find out by whom."

"Warren, let's start with you. Where did you go after dinner?" Alistair asked, his voice level.

"I went to my room as soon as I was certain that everyone was settled in. I wanted to make sure I was ready for an early start today. I ran into Valerie in the kitchen before I went to bed, and I said goodnight to her. She seemed fine. That was the last I saw of her. I remained in my room until the next morning."

"Can anyone confirm this?"

Warren shrugged. "No, of course not. I didn't know I was going to need an alibi."

"Err, speaking of Valerie being in the kitchen. I don't know if it was her, but around midnight I woke up and couldn't go back to sleep so I made myself some tea downstairs. The French doors were partly open and I heard voices outside. They belonged to a man and a woman, but I don't know much else. I didn't see anyone and I can't even be sure the female's voice belonged to Valerie."

Alistair raised an eyebrow as I saw the cogs in his head turn. The look he gave me made me believe he had just figured out why I had asked him about last night at the breakfast table.

I looked at my hands, unable to meet his eyes.

"Brenda, did you go outside at midnight?"

She startled visibly. "No, of course not."

"If that is true, then we should assume it was Valerie. Which one of you was she talking to?"

The three men all shrugged or shook their heads.

"Which means either one of you is lying because that's when you killed her, or it was someone else entirely," Alistair said. He flipped a page in his notebook.

"What about you, David? Where did you go after dinner?"

"I took a shower and was on my tablet for a while, then went down to the kitchen for a drink around ten and went up again. And no, I didn't run into anyone." His shoulders were tensed, and he avoided eye contact with Alistair.

"And we were rehearsing a couple of moments we'd act out for this weekend," Brenda said before Alistair could even ask. "Weren't we, darling?"

"Yes. We pretty much stayed in our room all night." Geoff nodded at Alistair.

"How convenient," Detective Black whispered in my ear.

"Aren't you all part of the same acting group?" I asked, my voice hoarse.

They all looked at me as if they'd forgotten I was there.

Geoff cleared his throat. "Well, yes. We're The Dramateers. Valerie was part of our group. She was a good actress."

"So you knew Valerie well," I said.

"We rehearse twice a week and we've done some performances," Geoff said again. I was guessing he was the leader.

"You weren't friends?"

His eyes widened. "Of course we were. She was a good friend to all of us."

I studied them. None of them looked terribly convinced of that. It could be because they were all in shock, but considering Valerie's behaviour, I wasn't so sure about that.

"Is it true she was strangled?" Warren asked.

Alistair was quiet for a moment. His eyes met mine. "We're not sure yet, but it appears so."

I winced.

"Oh, dear." Brenda touched her own neck as her nose wrinkled.

"That poor girl," Geoff muttered. "Her husband will be heartbroken."

"She was married? I didn't notice a ring," Alistair said.

"She was. His name was Johnny Cooke."

"I know it's not ideal, but for now I want you all to remain here. I still want to question you all individually over on the sofa by the fireplace. Miles, I'll speak with you first. And Maggie, after that I want to talk to you."

I nodded.

"Are you okay?" Eddie asked me quietly while the others were either lost in thought or chatting amongst themselves.

I leaned closer to him. "She had been strangled with my scarf," I whispered.

Eddie's eyes widened. "That's terrible."

"I know. Anyone could have grabbed it easily, but it really freaks me out that my scarf was the...murder weapon."

"Of course, it would freak me out too."

I glanced around at the members of the Dramateers. They looked worried and gloomy, but that didn't mean they were innocent. I knew better than anyone that looks could be deceiving.

"Oh yeah. I wouldn't trust them as far as I can throw them," Detective Black said.

WHEN IT WAS MY TURN, I walked all the way to the other side of the long room. Alistair had spoken with Miles, who briefly touched my arm in passing. It was now my turn to face the music.

Hugh was right next to Alistair, also with a notebook.

"Hey," I said, as I sat down opposite him.

"How are you feeling?" he asked me, concern mixed into his warm voice.

I shrugged and looked at my hands. "She was strangled with my scarf."

Hugh gasped and Alistair glared at him. "I just told you that," he said.

"Oh, right," Hugh said and checked his notes. "You did. Sorry."

Alistair turned his attention back to me. "Do you have any idea how that could have happened?" His voice was gentle, and I knew he didn't mean to imply anything, but I still felt a fresh wave of guilt.

"No. Warren took my coat and scarf just like he did for everyone, I assume. I haven't touched it since our first stroll in the garden."

"Could you go through what happened last night again?" he asked.

"Of course." I swallowed. "I woke up at midnight and couldn't sleep and decided to go to the kitchen and make some tea. I noticed it was cold and saw that one of the French doors was ajar. I heard two voices. A man's and a woman's. I couldn't tell who they belonged to and the kettle was making a lot of noise. I figured it was none of my business and left. I wouldn't have done that if I had any reason to think someone was in danger."

Alistair stopped writing and looked up at me. "We know that." He even added a smile.

It made me feel a little better. "Thank you." Then I glanced behind me at the dining room table where the others were.

"Friday night I saw Valerie in the garden with David. I don't know why, but if that was a regular thing with them, then maybe it was him she was talking to last night as well."

Alistair nodded slowly and wrote it down. "We'll take it into consideration." He cleared his throat. "Anyway, this is a police matter, so please do not concern yourself with this murder. If you remember anything helpful, don't hesitate to let us know." He had adopted a more professional and distant tone.

Detective Black popped up right behind him and shook his head. "Too late. She's already concerned," he said to Alistair, even though he couldn't hear him.

Eddie and Alistair had been—and still were—very worried for my safety, and I understood why they wouldn't want me to get my sleuth on, but still—this murder would haunt me until the killer was caught.

Chapter Ten

The rest of the day went by in a blur. I had taken Miles home with me because I didn't want him to have to be there with nothing but his thoughts and police tape in his garden. The Castlefield Book Club had already stopped by with baked goods to cheer us up—and mostly for gossip. Not that they were being insensitive, but information was power and they wanted this murder solved just as much as I did. They probably already assumed I'd be looking into it and they were probably eager to offer assistance, as they had in the past. Well, assistance was a bit of a stretch, but they tried.

I still couldn't help but wonder why Valerie had been killed that night, during a murder mystery weekend?

Plus, the way she had been killed implied that it was in a fit of anger. The killer literally grabbed what was closest at hand.

As the baker's wife, Olivia always had access to comfort food and she had brought delicious pastries which she practically thrust on me since word had already gotten out that I had tripped over the body. Her hair was short and looked messy today while she also had streaks of flour on her cheek.

"I still can't believe that poor girl actually died," Eleanor said as she helped Nancy bring in the tea.

"I can," Nancy said. "She enjoyed riling people up, that much was obvious."

Miles, Eddie and I had all taken a pastry, and as soon as the plate went on the coffee table, the pastries slowly disappeared into the vacuum that was known as Poppy. She ate like a sumo wrestler who needed to store fat. Not that Poppy was fat, quite the opposite. How she managed it, I don't know. If only I could adopt her metabolism.

"Not that she deserved to die," Eleanor said.

"Of course not," Nancy added. "I never said she did."

"Some people do," Ava said in her lovely Scottish accent. She always managed to make her blunt comments sound poetic. Well, almost.

"Ava," Eleanor scolded.

She shrugged. "Just saying what everyone's thinking."

"Not everyone has such a dark mind," Lily interjected.

"So you say," Ava muttered.

Jessica was sitting on the floor playing with Snowball. She had grabbed one of my balls of yarn and was pushing it towards Snowball while Phoebe observed it with a shaking head. She managed to look like a strict school teacher.

To my surprise, though, Snowball pushed around the ball of yarn with her little nose and hopped after it.

Conversation was beginning to drift away from the topic of murder as Lily tried to get Miles to go out with her single daughter while she used her latest invention: a tea spoon which doubled as a cookie holder. It was quite effective up until the part where you stirred and the cookie fell off.

I was relieved that they all provided a welcome distraction, but it was nice when they left and I was surrounded by a smaller group of people. The bigger the group of people around me, the more I would feel drained afterwards.

Funny that I didn't have that with fictional characters.

Eddie and Christina showed up with pizza around dinner time and all four of us were watching Netflix while eating. I was in between Christina and Miles while Eddie was in the armchair. Snowball was lying on her side by the fireplace. Occasionally her whiskers twitched. I couldn't help but wonder what she daydreamed about. Probably big carrots.

"Did you know that Eddie attended one of the Castlefield Book Club meetings?" Christina asked us with a grin.

"You did? Did you enjoy it?" I knew how weird those meetings could easily become. Half of the time they seriously discussed the books they'd read, but the other half was just...well, weird.

"I should have known what I was getting myself into," Eddie said, "but it just so happened that I'd read the book they were going to discuss, and I was curious if it would be fun."

I narrowed my eyes at him. "What book did you read?"

His freckled and pale skin turned red. "Shut up. Anyway," he started.

"Why is he turning red?" Miles whispered to me.

"Probably because it means he's read a really fluffy romance, but he doesn't want to admit it." This last part I said louder. "Even though romance is for everyone."

"I said shut up," he hissed at me. "Anyway, Phoebe and Jessica showed up first, but they were dressed as a block of cheese and a carton of milk."

I had heard about that. And no, it hadn't anything to do with it almost being Halloween.

"Why?" Miles asked.

"It turns out they were silently protesting," Eddie said.

"Protesting what?" Miles frowned.

"Dairy," I said.

He gaped like a fish, still not understanding.

"They like to protest things. It's...don't worry about it. Once you get to know them better, you'll understand." I flashed him a smile. The first time I had run into the neighbours, they were in fluorescent biking outfits with equally noticeable bikes and yelled at every car that drove by, trying to get people to cycle to work. Problem is, if you live in a remote village where people have to drive about fifty minutes to get to work, nobody is going to cycle.

"But...dairy?" Miles said.

"Then Eleanor and Nancy showed up with lemon tarts and Poppy followed not long thereafter and went straight for the food," Eddie continued. "Which is all very normal, especially since everyone else then trickled in and took their seats. They all had the book with them, and I reckoned we were about to start when Olivia suddenly started crying."

"Wait. Who's she again?" Miles asked.

"The baker's wife. Brown hair, always smiles."

"Right." We turned our attention back to Eddie, who was enjoying drawing the story out. At least, I guessed so, based on the glint in his eyes.

I hadn't heard this piece of gossip yet, so I was actually very curious as to what could make the lovely Olivia cry. The woman could smile through a funeral. Not because she wouldn't be upset, but because she always found beauty in everything. I admired that kind of strength.

"She said she suspects Stanley of cheating," Eddie said in a low voice.

I actually gasped. "No way, he would never."

"That's what Eleanor said, but then Ava said something not so friendly about men in general, to which Lily piled on and that just made the crying worse."

"Why does she think Stanley is cheating on her?" Christina asked. Apparently she also hadn't heard this part yet.

"She said that a few times this week he left late at night and when he came back he simply said he went for a walk." Eddie shrugged. "Could be true, right?"

"Yes, of course. Stanley loves her to bits." But with all the murders going on, I realised it was difficult to truly know someone. Maybe he was cheating. "What days did he go and what time?"

Eddie laughed. "I knew it. I knew you were going to look into it. Are you sure you can fit a suspected cheating case into your new murder case?" He raised an eyebrow in challenge.

"I—I never said I was investigating Valerie's murder."

"We all know you're going to do it," Eddie said.

"Yeah, we do," Christina said. Even Miles nodded.

"I promised you I wouldn't," I said to Eddie.

"But you want to anyway. I can see it in your eyes. Look, I'll help you."

My mouth dropped open. "What? But you're the one who said it was too dangerous."

"Not if I'm with you. I know how to kick ass now. I'll be your assistant." Eddie grinned.

"And I will help too. I need to do something," Miles said.

Yeah, I totally got that. I glanced at Christina.

She held up her hands. "Oh, no. I already had to cancel my date, and I'm not doing it again." She winked at me. "You kids have fun chasing a murderer."

Okay, she didn't have to say it like that.

Detective Black was in front of the fire. "Ooh, I feel tingly all over. This is going to be exciting."

I sighed. "Okay. We'll start tomorrow. Tonight, we relax."

Hopefully, it wouldn't be too long before we got to unwind again.

AFTER ALISTAIR HAD finished his questioning and did his due diligence, the actors were allowed to go home. They had to leave their details and obviously had to remain available for follow-up questions, but it meant they were able to resume their lives. This was beneficial to us because all their drama rehearsals were open to the public, and I also knew they had a performance next month. Rehearsals had already started before this weekend. Their next meeting, however, wouldn't be until Monday night, which meant that this weekend was reserved for some basic research.

AKA Facebook stalking.

"You know," Detective Black said, "If you make me a bit more inclined to use technology, I could use the Friendbook to gather clues."

"It's Facebook, and your apprehension towards technology is endearing and ensures that Mary can come up with some useful information. You're not a private detective, after all. You have colleagues."

He wrinkled his nose. "I suppose. It would be a lot easier if I was a private detective; there'd be less paperwork involved."

"I doubt that."

"Although you seem to have acquired colleagues as well." Detective Black smirked at me. He was looming over me while I was on a meditation cushion next to the coffee table in the living room. I had on a snug orange jumper and warm, grey jogging trousers. Next to me was a steaming mug of tea and no biscuits (yay, self-control!) while Snowball was running around. Christina was downstairs working at The Wicked Bookworm but only until lunch time. Then she had her date with the guy she hadn't told me anything about yet.

I would cover her afternoon shift, which meant I only had this morning to do some snooping. I did welcome the distraction that working at my bookshop provided.

In my notebook, I had written down all the names of the people involved in the murder mystery weekend apart from myself. Then I crossed out Alistair, Miles and Eddie. I mean, Alistair was definitely out, and I knew Eddie well enough. I could choose to be paranoid and leave him on the list, but I was pretty damn certain Miles would never strangle someone with my scarf.

I started with Geoff Jones. His personal Facebook page pretty much consisted of posts from the Facebook page for The Dramateers. I clicked on it. He and his wife Brenda had started their little acting group The Dramateers. They met at a theatre in Woolfield on Mondays, Wednesdays and Fridays. It seemed they were all very passionate about acting if they met that many times.

"Check the photos," Detective Black said. "No doubt we'll be able to spot lingering gazes, spiteful glances and even worse than that: food pictures." He shuddered. "Food should be eaten, not photographed."

I wholeheartedly agreed, but it seemed that the pictures for the drama club were exactly what I was looking for. There were a lot taken on nights they had performed, but also during rehearsals. I was more interested in the behind the scenes photos. That's when people lowered their guard.

They looked like normal pictures of actors rehearsing. Valerie was only in the background in some of them, writing in a notebook. There were a few pictures that stood out to me because in two separate ones, Valerie had her hand on David and Geoff's arms and was laughing at something they'd said. It looked like she had been flirting with both of them. There was also a picture where Valerie was being silly and everyone else was smiling as they watched her. Everyone but Brenda.

"Jealousy doesn't have to be about love," Detective Black said as he leaned forward.

I frowned and went back to check out the posts. After some scrolling, I found what I was looking for. Valerie had the lead role in their upcoming play called *Worse for Wear*. Well, obviously not anymore.

I clicked on a link that led to the website for The Drama-teers. "Bingo," I said as I scrolled through the info on their last four plays. "Every lead role went to Valerie. I'm fairly sure Geoff decides on the roles, so Brenda wouldn't be too happy about that, I reckon. Hell, maybe even the guys weren't too happy about it. It was, after all, a man she had been talking with."

"Still. It is possible that the man she spoke with left quickly after you did and the killer showed up after that," Detective Black said.

I pursed my lips. He had a point. It was unlikely, but very possible. There could have even been a total of three people there. Just because I had heard a woman's voice and a man's, didn't mean they were the only people.

"And the plot thickens," I said as I scribbled in my notebook.

Chapter Eleven

Around noon, I went downstairs to relieve Christina. She went up to change her outfit and freshen up before her date arrived while I slipped behind the counter and rang up a few customers. All of them wanted to know more about this new murder, but I was very good at giving them the old runaround and instead I started talking about the migration patterns of monarch butterflies. I once had to do a presentation about that and for some reason remembered the info still.

That sent them scurrying off with their newly purchased books which they possibly got just to hear some gossip. Okay, maybe it hadn't been a good idea to scare them off then, but it just didn't feel right to tell strangers about it as if it was... entertainment. The book club ladies were genuinely disturbed, and yes, they liked gossip, but discussing a murder case wasn't the same as discussing Winnie Harolds DIY hair colouring that resulted in a startling amount of hair loss. Now she wore a wig that made her look like a hedgehog.

"Excuse me," a man's voice said.

I looked around as there was nobody in front of the counter. Oh wait, a hand waved above it, forcing me to lean over.

"Hi." A little person stared up at me. He was dressed in a nice black pullover that brought out his startling blue eyes. The single rose in his other hand was the only clue I needed to deduce that this was Christina's date.

"Oh, hi. Sorry, I didn't see you." I came out from behind the counter.

"That's okay. I get that a lot." He grinned at me and stuck out his hand. "I'm Bill. I'm Christina's date."

"Nice to meet you." I leaned forward and shook his hand. "Maggie Matthews. I'm the bookshop owner and both friend and flatmate of Christina."

"In that case, I have to make sure I stay on your good side. I'd offer this rose, but it's for Christina."

I laughed. "That's okay. If you really want to get on my good side, get me anything food related and I'll be putty in your hands."

"I'll keep that in mind."

Just then, Christina appeared with a goofy smile on her face and in a lovely long-sleeved dress that accentuated her curves. She also wore her leather jacket, again managing to look both classy and cool.

After a few polite words, they went off into the wild to enjoy their date. I could only hope they would not cross paths with the most dangerous creature in this village: Pandora.

Eddie entered for his shift, walking in at the same time as Alistair. They chatted briefly before Eddie went over to Brian who was working on a display for a new sci-fi book. He once managed to set a display on fire, so I was glad that Eddie went over to help him. It was quiet now anyway.

"Hey," Alistair said. Lines around his dark eyes appeared as he smiled.

"Hey."

Next to me, Detective Black made kissing noises.

"Want some tea and talk about murder?"

He raised an eyebrow. "Tea would be lovely."

SNOWBALL WAS ON ALISTAIR'S lap when I returned with the tea and biscuits. I had promised myself I could have one biscuit when there were visitors. Not that I'd only brought out two biscuits. I wasn't a monster.

"How are you feeling?" Alistair asked when I sat next to him.

"I'm feeling better now. Though it may be a while before I wear a scarf."

"I understand. I do hope you don't feel responsible in some way." He eyed me with a dash of concern.

"Wouldn't you?"

"Yes. That's why I'm asking." He smiled at me, though there was still that bit of concern in his expression. "You are not in control of the actions of others."

"Neither are you," I said.

"We're not talking about me right now."

"I wish we were," I mumbled.

Alistair chuckled and was about to say something when I held up my hand.

"Don't worry. I think I'm over the initial shock. I would feel infinitely better if you have a clue about who the killer is." I raised my eyebrows expectantly.

"And if I don't know, it means you'll start investigating, right?" He raised his eyebrow right back.

I shrugged. "Eddie seems to think so."

"With your track record, can you blame him? Look, I understand it's especially tempting considering how she was killed, but I don't like the idea of you putting yourself in harm's way. Again."

"I know I scared you with the last investigation, but as you well remember, I had been minding my own business when I was attacked. It just goes to show that nowhere is really safe. I could get hit by a bus or fall down the stairs."

This only made Alistair's eyebrows rise towards his hairline.

"Though I'm sure that won't happen. We all gotta do what we gotta do. I can hardly live in fear all the time. Besides, Eddie and Miles said they'd help me. It means I won't be alone. Now, tell me what you found out. Please." There really was no need to worry. The only plan I had was to visit The Dramateers. I wasn't even sure if I'd find out anything important.

"Fine. I will tell you."

I leaned forward. "Go on."

"After we have lunch. Follow me." He got up and held out his hand while still holding Snowball in his other arm.

I took it and got up as well.

Before we went out, I put Snowball in her cage and then grabbed my coat. His Beetle was parked at the back of the bookshop and we got in to go off to a mysterious location; he wouldn't tell me where.

Ten minutes later we stopped at the side of a dirt path in the woods. There was a large field with a lone tree in the middle. The grass wasn't too tall, and there were only a few fallen leaves that had been blown over from the forest. Alistair went to the back of the car and retrieved a picnic basket and a blanket.

"Here," he said as he handed me the blanket.

"We're having a picnic?" I stared at the clouds, trying to discern if it was going to rain.

"Don't worry. The forecast is on our side. Come on." He made his way to the tree as I followed him, still wrapping my head around it.

"I never would have thought you like to live so dangerously." I placed the blanket on the grass and sat down while Alistair unpacked the picnic basket and handed me a plate with a wrapped sandwich that he'd gotten from Stanley.

"Aha, you didn't even make the lunch yourself, huh?" I said.

Alistair grinned. "Nah, you're not worth that much trouble."

I lightly punched Alistair's arm.

"It seems *you* like to live dangerously if you go around assaulting police detectives."

I couldn't help but laugh. "This is really nice of you."

He shrugged. "It was a fun weekend, but the ending kind of ruined it. I wanted to do something nice and take your mind off things."

"I appreciate that. A lot."

Alistair handed me a glass of grape juice, since he knew I liked that, and took out several lunch boxes filled with food. Grapes, biscuits, cake, strawberries, and even cheese and crackers. Hadn't I told him I wanted to lose a few pounds?

"Yes," Detective Black said, "And he told you you were perfect."

Right.

I blushed.

It was touching to know he had gone out of his way to make this for me. There was a burst of nervous energy that spread across my chest as I started to fumble with my sleeve.

"What is it?" Alistair narrowed his eyes.

Why did he have to be so observant? Or perhaps that was a good thing.

"I just wanted to say something." I cleared my throat. "I think maybe, you know, I was a bit scared to date you. I mean, a lot of important people in my life have sort of...left, and you are kind of special to me. I guess I was afraid that I'd lose you too."

I managed to look into his eyes, gauging his reaction.

He smiled.

"Why are you smiling?"

"Because now I don't feel so bad about being terrified myself. I guess after things went wrong with Christina and how I lost myself in London, I was really worried I would screw things up with you, so I was relieved when we decided to stay friends."

"But don't you feel it's such a shame to be led by fear? I feel so cowardly."

"Trust me, you're not cowardly at all. But I suppose we could... hang out. We don't have to mention dates, but we can spend more time together and see what happens. No pressure." His tone sounded light, but there was an eagerness in his eyes that matched what I was feeling.

"Okay. Sure," I said in a matching tone.

"Yet, on the inside you are screaming," Detective Black said.

It was more like I was doing a happy dance, but whatever.

We continued to eat our sandwiches while I told Alistair about the tricks I'd taught Snowball. She could jump over my arm, run in a circle, and stand on her back legs. Alistair was suitably impressed and then told me about the tricks he'd taught his dog. He even went so far as to demonstrate the tricks after I pretended not to understand his explanation. Although I was pretty sure he knew I was pretending and was just using it to make me laugh.

The sandwiches were delicious and afterwards I moved on to the grapes. Alistair was on his side. He had finished eating and was just staring at my face.

"So you planned this picnic to cheer me up, huh?" I asked.

He shrugged with one shoulder. "Is it working?"

"It is."

He smiled. "Good."

I really liked his smile. It seemed he was showing it to me more and more.

"How's your therapy going?" I wasn't entirely sure if he was still going, but he hadn't told me otherwise.

"Good. I'm seeing her less and less, which is a good sign." His smile was now gone and replaced by a more guarded expression.

I understood that. When he and Christina had been dating, he hadn't communicated with her at all. The fact that he had informed me about his therapist—though he did that by necessity—was already a big step. I just hoped that one day he'd feel comfortable enough to tell me anything he wanted. Including telling me about his dead partner and the suspect he was forced to kill in self-defence.

"I'll tell you about it some other time," he said. "I think now you've earned your reward."

My eyes lit up. "My reward? Is it more food?"

He bit his lip, trying to keep a smile from slipping out. He was not successful. "I thought you wanted to know more about the murder."

"Oh, yeah. I do. Tell me." He had my undivided attention.

Okay, maybe a part of me was still on the grapes. They were really good.

"They all say that they were in bed around the time that the murder must have occurred. Based on your statement, the victim was killed after two. Geoff and Brenda can vouch for each other, but of course they could be lying. And Warren and David don't have anyone to vouch for their whereabouts. It doesn't mean they did it, of course. There are no mysterious text messages on her phone but there were angry messages exchanged between her and her husband. We informed him this morning. He didn't take it well."

"Maybe you can find out a little bit about their relationship," I said.

"Why do you say that?"

"I think Valerie was a bit of a flirt with some of the other members of the drama club as well. I saw some pictures on the website of The Dramateers and it seemed all the guys were taken with her. She's also been the lead in the last few plays. I'm going to visit them tonight to see if I can pick up some stuff. Don't worry, I'll bring back-up." I winked at him.

"It could have been someone else entirely," Alistair said.

"I know. I'm keeping an open mind."

"Just be careful."

I reached over and squeezed his hand. "And you. Thank you for the picnic. It was really nice of you."

"That's what friends are for."

Detective Black sighed heavily in the background.

Chapter Twelve

Since Nancy was spending more and more time with Gus, it meant that Emblyn was alone in the shop. She was doing quite well for a recent part-time employee and loved working in my aunt's occult shop, but I still checked up on her regularly. It was good to know that Nancy finally trusted her enough to run her shop without her there, especially since they met because Emblyn had stolen candles from her.

First I hit the bakery to get some muffins for Emblyn—I would eat only one—and was looking forward to seeing all the delicious baked goods. I would enjoy looking at them just as much as eating them. Oh, who was I kidding?

It was quiet in the bakery and Stanley was in the back while Olivia was selling some cheesecake slices to—I moved to the side to get a better look of the woman's face—ah, Carry. She owned the local jewellery shop called Put a Ring on It. We both shared a love for cheesecake and we had almost gotten into a fight over the last slice of Stanley's strawberry cheesecake a few months ago. It hadn't been very dignified.

At least we had made up since then.

"Oh, hi, Molly," Carry said with a smile.

Okay, never mind.

"Hello, Carly." Two could play that game.

Her smile vanished and she left with her nose in the air.

Olivia shook her head in dismay. "If I'd known cheesecake would cause such problems, I would have told Stanley not to make it."

"Don't you dare ever say such a horrible thing ever again," I said in mock anger.

Olivia chuckled, but then her features turned serious and she glanced over her shoulder. She scuttled from behind the counter and clasped my hands in hers.

"I want to hire you," she said.

I frowned. "To write?"

"No, of course not. To investigate."

"Why would you—"

"I think Stanley is cheating on me," she whispered.

"Oh, no. I'm sure that's not true." So what Eddie had told me really was true. Not that I had doubted him, but part of me had hoped. I liked things to be the way they were supposed to be. Olivia had been married before, to a man who liked to hit her. When she met Stanley it had transformed her from a timid, heartbroken woman to the cheerful and happy Olivia that had been buried inside.

"Yes, yes, so everyone keeps saying. But every Tuesday and Thursday evening he disappears for two hours. He says he's going for a walk, but I'm not stupid. I tried following him once myself, but one of my neighbours saw me and started talking and I couldn't break away. It's probably a good thing. I don't know how I would have reacted if I'd seen him with another woman." Her eyes filled with tears.

"Okay, calm down. Don't worry. I'll help you. But are you sure you don't just want to ask him? I mean, this is Stanley we are talking about."

She shook her head. "No. I know that men can be good at lying. I don't want to think of Stan as being one of those men, but I won't rest until someone sees it with their own eyes."

"It's possible it's something else entirely."

"I know, bu—"

There were shuffling sounds as Stanley emerged from the back. "Oh, hey Mags, hadn't seen you."

"Hi, Stanley. I was just showing Olivia my new lipstick."

"You're not wearing any," Olivia whispered with a hint of panic.

Oh, right.

"It looks nice," Stanley said as he put some doughnuts in the front window. He whistled a tune as he disappeared into the back again.

"Thank goodness he's as observant as a sleeping goldfish."

I laughed.

"Now, what can I get you?"

I CARRIED THE BOX OF muffins to The Wicked Bookworm so I could give one to Eddie and Brian before sharing them with Emblyn. I was looking forward to seeing her. I had checked up on her, but Nancy's shop was always busy this month, so I hadn't talked to her as much as I wanted in the past two weeks. Now was the perfect time. I could edit later, and tonight I'd be able to sleuth. And that was assuming the visit to The Dramateers would lead to anything.

Eddie was ringing up a customer and gave me a cheery greeting, which I returned. He looked particularly grateful when I placed the muffin near him. I went through the curtain behind the counter. The small space between our shops was filled with a kitchenette and a table with two chairs. Just as I was about to push the curtain open on the other side, I heard a young man's voice.

"Come on. It will be fun, I promise," the guy said.

"I don't know. It sounds like trouble." Emblyn's voice was soft and the words hesitant. She clearly didn't want to disappoint him.

Was she seeing anyone? She hadn't mentioned it. Then again, when we spoke, she usually wanted to know what was happening with me and Alistair. Not that I'd ever had any juicy details for her. All the excitement happened in my books.

I opened the curtain and visibly startled the guy who was probably one or two years older than Emblyn. I guessed he was eighteen or something. He had shoulder length brown hair and a lip piercing.

"Hello," I said as I bent down to pet Bailey, Nancy's Border terrier, who let out an excited bark.

"Oh, Maggie. Hi. I didn't see you," Emblyn said. She had changed the pink and purple streaks in her dark curls for orange and red. Her makeup was heavier than usual. Was it because of him?

"I don't think we've met," I said with a bit more steel than I had intended.

Emblyn shifted her weight and smiled, but it was a nervous smile. "This is Elijah. Elijah, this is Maggie. She owns the bookshop next door and she's a writer."

I took a step closer to the counter and held out my hand. When he took it, I squeezed firmly. "Nice to meet you."

"And you," he said, then turned to Emblyn. "I gotta go. See you later."

"Yeah. See you."

We both watched him go.

"The boy needs to wear a belt," I said. "I don't get the fashion sense of teens these days."

I figured that would earn me a smile from Emblyn, but she just blinked at me.

"Okay. Who is he and what was he talking about?" I figured I'd get straight to the point.

"He's sort of my almost-boyfriend."

Whatever that meant.

"Is that like my almost-exercising? When I just look up yoga studios, basically."

She shrugged.

"And the answer to the second question?"

"He was just talking about a party. That's all."

I leaned against the counter and crossed my arms. "And you don't want to go? You don't have to if you don't want to. Especially if it's going to be *trouble*."

She flinched at that last word. "It's not. It's not. I just said the wrong word."

"Like when I say cheesecake instead of salad?"

Still no smile. Tough crowd.

"It's fine, Maggie. You're not my mother." She glanced up at me as if to see if that had wounded me.

It hadn't. I just knew that her dad was a busy corporate lawyer and her mother—well, she talked about her as much as I talked about mine. Whatever was going on there, it wasn't anything good. Via the grapevine, I had heard that her parents were officially still together but her mother worked so much that she was barely home. Either way, with Nancy distracted by Gus, I felt even more inclined to look out for Emblyn. I didn't want her to be lonely, and I certainly didn't want her to get into trouble.

Perhaps it was time for a little bonding.

"You know. I have a case I'm working on."

Her eyes lit up at that. "The murder?"

I couldn't stop a shiver going through my body. "No."

"Oh." Her shoulders sagged.

Man, she loved mysteries almost as much as I did.

"Can you keep a secret?"

"Of course." She nodded eagerly.

"Olivia thinks Stanley might be having an affair. And I could use an assistant on this delicate matter. We're going to have to talk to Olivia and then shadow Stanley."

"Like follow him? With binoculars?"

I imagined what that would look like and the many strange looks we'd get. "Maybe not binoculars, but yeah, we'll definitely need to follow him. Maybe take some pictures. Have snacks in-between."

"Okay. I'm in. When do we start?"

"Tomorrow night."

"Okay. This is so exciting." A wide grin slid across her face.

A potential cheating spouse made her smile.

Teens, I will never understand them.

"Should I bring anything?" Then she snapped her fingers as she realised what my answer would be.

"Snacks," we said simultaneously.

Chapter Thirteen

The rest of the afternoon I worked on my edits because work still had to be done, even if it involved fictional murders and was therefore maybe not as important as a real one.

"I beg to differ," Detective Black said in an acerbic tone.

Around five o'clock, I went out through the back of my shop and made my way over to the Pembroke. Eddie had mentioned that last night he and Miles stayed up late playing video games and that Miles had crashed on Eddie's sofa. I was glad that he'd had a nice distraction and didn't have to sleep in that mansion on his own, but I felt uneasy at the thought of him being there now.

Miles had lived here for about six months, but he still hadn't fully immersed himself into village life. Which also meant he hadn't yet fully experienced the charms of this village. I didn't want him to associate tragedy and murder with the place that was now his home.

Hence, I was a woman on a mission.

I was panting heavily by the time he opened one of the doors. He was dressed more casually in a navy pullover and dark trousers.

"Maggie. What a pleasant surprise," he said, sounding as if he meant it.

I liked that about him. He was always polite and it didn't come across as forced. I imagined he could ruthlessly undermine any witness on the stand in that same tone. I'd never said it to him, but I fiercely admired him.

"We're having dinner at the pub," I said cheerfully.

"We are?" A line appeared at the corner of his lips as he came close to smirking.

"Oh, yes. Are you ready?"

He patted his trouser pocket. "Yes." Then he stepped outside and locked the door before holding out his arm.

I took it.

"Why were you panting when I answered the door?" he asked.

"I saw Pandora," I said. "Again. I think she's waiting for me to visit you so she can pounce and mur—never mind." I was here to cheer him up, not to make him think about murder. *Great going, Maggie.*

"That monstrous being should be introduced to a preheated oven," Miles said coldly.

I laughed before I could stop myself. "I don't think anything could stop her. Not even an oven."

We kept looking over our shoulders, making sure Pandora wasn't anywhere in the vicinity as we moved across the cobbled streets. Instead of heading to the pub, I took Miles past the church and in a different direction.

"Where are we going? Are we picking up Alistair?" he asked.

"No. First we're visiting Beth, our oldest resident. She's lovely and I don't believe you've had the honour of meeting her."

He glanced at me. "I do know of her. I lived here as a child, remember? Not that I ever recall meeting her. Why are you introducing us now?"

"Why not?" I said, keeping my tone light.

He said nothing, but his expression told me he knew. And he would be right, but the effect of cheering someone up lessens when you tell them you're cheering them up.

We arrived at the cottage opposite Alistair's. It was white with windows on either side of the front door. There were carved pumpkins along the short path to her house, and I happened to know that Eleanor had carved them for her. She also took care of her garden in summer and spring.

Normally, I'd bring books with me, but I had given her a fresh batch of literature a couple of days ago. My present today would be Miles and his dazzling smile. I'm sure she would appreciate that.

I picked up the key from under the flower pot that was pushed off to the side to make room for the pumpkins.

"She really shouldn't keep her key there," Miles said with a hint of indignation. "She could be robbed or mur—" his voice trailed off. It was the first sign he'd given me that he really didn't want to be reminded of the murder. He was a criminal attorney and I'm sure he was used to a lot, but it's different when there's a corpse in your own garden.

It made me feel relieved to know I was right trying to cheer him up but worried at the same time.

A visit to Beth and a pub meal would definitely help.

I was about to tell him he had nothing to worry about and that this village was safe, but then realised how stupid that would sound. Maybe it was time to make copies of the key for ourselves instead of leaving out the key under the pot.

Still, I liked to think that this village was safe, warm, and cosy. Even if a few murders had taken place.

"You're right," I said quietly, then unlocked the door. Before stepping in, I turned to Miles. "Sometimes Beth is a bit forgetful, but just go along with things. She'll like meeting you regardless of her state, I promise."

At this, he gave a rather sweet smile. "And I will be glad to meet her."

"Hello, Beth. It's Maggie," I called out as I entered her cottage. It smelt like lemon, which meant someone had come round to clean for her. It would be either Eleanor or Olivia. Maybe even Lily. Since she was the inventor of useless items such as a mop that was also a hoover, she had been known to drop by and help Beth out. Apparently she didn't let the fact that she only cared about herself stop her from being kind to Beth. She did let it stop her from being kind to anyone else.

Okay. Sometimes she was nice.

"Arr." It came from the kitchen.

"Oh, oh. Whatever that sound meant, it means she's probably not her usual self," I said to Miles.

He followed dutifully behind me, refraining from making any comments. I appreciated that because I felt nervous about what I'd find. So far it was all harmless. She usually believed she was someone else based on a TV programme she'd watched—I had therefore disconnected her TV a long time ago—or a book she'd read—which is why I only gave her cheerful, happy books—or even stories she's heard.

We entered the kitchen and Beth—hundred and two years old—was standing on her dining room table with an eye patch over her left eye and a broom in her hand.

"Ahoy, mateys!" she said with a grin on her face.

I wasn't sure if I'd ever seen her grin, but I liked how cocky it made her look.

"Hello, Captain," I said calmly while panic mode was officially engaged inside my head.

I guess my calm facade wasn't fool proof, because Miles put his hand on my lower back. "Permission to come aboard?" he asked.

Wow. He really was taking my advice to heart. Most people—actually, everyone except for Eleanor and me—always tried to get Beth to calm down or distract her during one of her episodes. I had expected Miles to want to do the same, but he seemed perfectly amused as he smiled up at her, a twinkle in his eyes.

Beth eyed him up and down. "Permission granted."

Miles turned one of the chairs sideways and held out his hand for me.

I shot him a grateful look and stepped onto the chair and then the table. Beth handed me the broom. "Keep rowing or those bastards will catch up to us."

My jaw dropped. Beth would scowl at me even if I so much as said 'blast.'

Miles dashed into the kitchen and returned with a near empty kitchen roll. He then joined us on the table and used the kitchen roll to pretend to peer into the distance. "They're catching up to us, Captain. What's the plan?"

Beth hesitated. "We'll lower the sails and lead them to those cliffs. I've got an idea."

Miles saluted her while I was still rowing...with the broom. If it was a real pirate ship then why would I need to row? Also, where had she gotten the eye—never mind. Halloween. There were costumes for sale pretty much everywhere in this village.

Our riveting chase lasted about ten minutes, just long enough for us to lead the enemy ship to the cliffs and then do a quick turn. Then Beth calmly removed her eye patch, turned to Miles and said, "Who are you? And why are you on my dining room table?"

"Spider," I said quickly.

She turned around and her eyes softened. "Maggie, dear. What are you—wait, did you say spider?"

"It's okay, Miles took care of it."

He helped us both get down to the floor before I officially introduced them.

"Beth, this is Miles, a good friend of mine."

"How nice to meet you, young man. You are very hand-some," she said without blushing.

"And you are very beautiful," he said and kissed the back of her hand.

She giggled like a school girl and her cheeks turned pink.

Nobody stood a chance when Miles turned on the charm.

"Why don't you sit down and I'll make us all some tea," I said.

"And bring out some brownies as well. Eleanor brought them today." Beth started walking towards the kitchen, clearly changing her mind about me being the hostess.

"No, no. You just relax. I'll take care of it, really." I smiled and gently nudged her towards Miles.

He held out his arm and that sealed the deal. They walked off as Beth fired off questions about his job, whether or not he was single, what his hobbies were and other questions.

A few minutes later I walked out with a tray filled with three cups and a teapot as well as three brownies. Much to my dismay, she was telling Miles about the time that I was fourteen and helped Beth in her back garden when I was chased by a dragonfly and ran screaming.

"At the time it was scary," I grumbled as I poured them all a cup of tea.

"Well," Miles said, "I'd never thought I'd be running for my life from a chicken so there's that."

Beth waved a hand. "Oh, she's just lonely. That's all."

I raised an eyebrow. *Yes, I'm sure Pandora just wants to braid our hair and have a tea party with us. Right before she eats us.*

"Oh, that reminds me, Maggie. How is that detective?" Miles chuckled.

I glared at him. "Alistair is doing well."

"But you're not dating yet?" She eyed Miles and then looked at me meaningfully.

"No, we're not and no, it has nothing to do with Miles."

She sighed and leaned back. "You know, people are too hesitant these days. I'm not saying you should get married straight away like they did in my days, but it would be nice to see people go for what they want."

"Hmm. I always figured you were someone like that," Miles said to me. "Seeing as how you so fearlessly go after murderers."

"I can understand why," Beth said. "Maggie has had some bad luck in the past. But you shouldn't let that hold you back, love."

I swallowed and nodded.

Miles was studying me, but I couldn't make eye contact. Instead I focussed on my tea.

"And you, Miles? Do you have any plans for the future?" Beth asked.

"No. I was engaged once."

I nearly spat out my tea and instead it went down the wrong pipe. My eyes started watering as I started coughing.

Miles scooted over and gently patted me on the back. "Don't think marriage is quite for me," he continued.

"It's very good that you know that about yourself. But marriage is no different than dating someone. I mean, these days you move in with each other before getting married and it's really just the same thing."

Sure. Don't mind me dying over here.

"Your face has gone red," Detective Black said, chuckling.

"Yes, well, I'm not sure if I want someone living with me either," Miles said.

"Why not?" I said in a grainy voice.

"It's just easier on my own." He stopped patting my back, and I managed to compose myself.

"You know, that probably comes from fear as well," I said. "You may be used to having things your way but a little disruption can be good."

"Perhaps. Who knows what the future holds?"

Hopefully, the future will hand us the killer on a silver platter.

"Oh, but that wouldn't be as fun," Detective Black said.

Chapter Fourteen

The Rose was also decorated for Halloween. Along the bar were orange and black flags and fake pumpkins were put on the corner of the bar. From the ceiling hung flags in the shapes of ghosts and bats, and Halloween-themed music was playing in the background. It was also packed since it was a Saturday, but we managed to find a table in the back.

We ordered fish and chips and drinks.

"So you don't have the best track record with men," Miles said after a comfortable silence.

I gave him a wry smile. "I figured you would remember that."

"It's an interesting piece of information." He smirked.

"How so?"

"It might explain why you haven't gone after Alistair."

I leaned back and folded my arms. "I haven't gone after him because Christina is my friend." Even if I had managed to tell Alistair the truth, I wasn't sure if I could tell anyone else.

He raised an eyebrow. "Did she say she didn't want you to date her ex?"

I bit my lip. "No. Quite the opposite."

His expression couldn't have been more smug.

"I don't think I like you anymore."

He laughed. "Go on. Tell me about your experiences with love. You've got me curious now."

"It's not that exciting, I promise."

"Stop stalling."

He really wasn't going to let this go, was he? Then again, if I really didn't want to talk about it, I wouldn't have. I had already gone over my romantic history with Christina—and she with me—and it had only made our friendship stronger. I wanted the same with Miles, yet I found myself hesitant. Was it because he was a man? Why would that matter? It's not like I was ashamed of my dating history. My bad luck with love was hardly my fault. It wasn't as if I had purposely sought out men who were going to hurt and leave me.

Just like my parents.

Okay, let's not go there.

It had already been difficult enough to tell Alistair I was afraid of dating him.

I shifted in my seat. "I had my first official boyfriend when I was twenty-three. We dated for a few months, but he said he wasn't feeling it. We said we'd try, but the very next time I saw him, he said that it still hadn't improved. I don't know why he thought that not seeing each other was trying, and when I asked him questions about how he felt about me, he basically described being in love with me. I just think he got into his own head and compared me to a previous relationship. Either way, I was not sad at all when that ended. Probably a bit relieved when I realised he wasn't willing to fight for me. Then I had a relationship with a guy who cheated on me and didn't even seem to care that much about apologising, and then there was Connor. He was special."

Miles quirked an eyebrow. "How so?"

"I thought he was the one. I was deeply and madly in love with him from the moment I met him."

"Ah. So love at first sight exists. Who knew?" Miles said as he rested his chin on his fist.

"It really does, but it's not all it's cracked up to be. I mean, despite those intense feelings that we both shared, it wasn't meant to be."

"You're really going to leave me hanging? Come on, what happened?"

I sighed. "Fine. It's nothing special. It's just that—well, I've never told anyone this, but he actually proposed to me." I waited for a dramatic gasp, but Miles just nodded and waited for me to continue. "But the next day he got a job offer. In Scotland. And he took it without even talking to me about it. He just assumed I'd go with him and when I said this was my home, he acted insulted. He basically implied I was *just* a bookshop owner and writer. And that I could go with him and it wouldn't be a huge sacrifice." I felt the disappointment and pain well up again. Usually when I felt this way I cracked a joke, but I had a feeling Miles would see right through that.

"Sounds like he took you for granted."

"I guess. It doesn't matter. It ended in a huge fight and I threw his briefcase out of the window."

Miles laughed so hard he actually snorted.

I couldn't help but laugh as well. "Why is that so funny?"

"Because I didn't think you would do something so volatile. You're so sweet."

"You forget who my aunt is. And also, just because I am sweet, doesn't mean I can't stand up for myself. Trust me, he totally deserved to have his briefcase thrown out of my window.

It was just lucky that nobody got hurt. Afterwards I felt very stupid."

"This village puts up with Pandora, so I'm sure a flying suitcase doesn't really matter much. Besides, as you said, nobody got hurt." Miles chuckled as he was probably picturing it again.

Except me.

"Anyway, what about you? Were you also engaged for just one day? Or did this last longer?"

Miles's grin disappeared and he cleared his throat. "It lasted a bit longer. My parents had picked her out and set us up. I went along with it because it's what I did back then. And I liked her, but I didn't love her. When I realised that, it was already too late and I ended up hurting her."

"Does Alistair know about this? Is she the reason you moved here?"

"I mentioned the relationship to Alistair but didn't explicitly mention we were engaged. I didn't want to talk about it then. And in a way she was the reason I moved here. I suppose the real reason was my parents, and me wanting to get away from their influence." He shot me a look. "As I'm sure you can understand."

"Oh yeah. One meeting was all it took for me to understand. No offence, but I hope I never see your parents again. Do they still think we're dating?"

One corner of his mouth turned up. "Oh, yes."

I chuckled. "Serves your dad right."

"Indeed."

When our food came, I shared some anecdotes with Miles, like how my aunt Nancy had once convinced Phoebe and Jessica that their cottages were being haunted by the ghosts of sheep. Miles hadn't spent much time with my aunt yet, but I figured it wouldn't hurt him to know what he would be dealing with.

"And how did your aunt lose her eye again?" he asked.

"Golfing accident."

His eyes widened. "Really?"

"No."

Another charming smile graced his face. "Are you going to tell me what really happened?"

"Don't fall for it," Detective Black said. "He's lulling you into a false sense of security."

I smiled back. "It was an accident with the washing machine."

He raised an eyebrow.

"No, wait. It happened at a Japanese restaurant. Chopsticks."

"You know what I like about you?"

"What?"

"There's never a dull moment with you."

WE STAYED FOR DRINKS as well, which is when Eddie joined us. He was going to tag along to the rehearsal of The Dramateers. Basically, I had two bodyguards.

"Three," Detective Black said over a fake cough.

Three.

The drive took a little over twenty minutes. The Dramateers—Geoff—had rented a small theatre to rehearse and perform in. We arrived a little late on purpose. There were four cars in the small parking space next to the building.

When we entered the theatre, there wasn't anyone to greet us and we went straight through to the double doors that led to the seats and stage. The Dramateers were already on the small stage with Geoff standing in front of the others.

Warren was the first to spot us. "An audience during rehearsals, we usually don't get those."

The others followed his gaze and apart from a cheery wave from David, the others didn't seem bothered either way. Warren immediately returned to some warming up movements—was he going to dance?—and Brenda was staring into a small handheld mirror while muttering to herself.

"They are all dressed in black," I said. "Do you think that's on purpose?"

"Probably. What is this play about?" Eddie asked.

"I have no clue."

"Are we ready?" Geoff hurried onto the stage.

Brenda put away the handheld mirror and instead picked up a pink ribbon that she started dancing with.

Oh, dear.

"A woman's cycle," she started.

Oh, dear. Oh, dear. Oh, dear.

"Nope," Eddie said as he shook his head.

"What? Are you not comfortable with a woman's cycle?" I asked.

Miles sniggered.

"Bicycle, sure, but the other...Err..." His voice trailed off and instead he produced some random high-pitched noises.

I laughed, but not loud enough to make the actors think I was laughing at them.

Brenda was now holding a pink rose. I had missed part of what she had been saying, but I had to remind myself I wasn't actually here to see them act. I was here to pick up on clues.

Hopefully, they would show up.

"If only you could lure them with food," Detective Black said as he lounged in one of the chairs in front of me. "Kind of like how you are so easily lured with food."

I narrowed my eyes at him.

Just as David and Warren started twirling around Brenda with cauliflowers, a door slammed open at the side of the stage.

A man with large biceps and a wild look in his dark eyes stormed onto the stage.

"Which one of you killed my Val? Which one of you bastards did it?" He looked about ready to strangle someone himself.

Everyone was frozen for a moment and then Geoff stepped forward.

"Johnny, we are so sorry for your loss. Why don't you come backstage and we'll make you some tea. I can even sing you a song. It always puts my wife to sleep."

Brenda snorted, then coughed to hide the indelicate slip.

"I don't want to bloody sleep, you tosser. I want to know who murdered my wife!"

Miles leaned closer to me. "I just texted Alistair. I have the feeling we might need him."

Johnny lunged towards Geoff, who let out a shriek.

Chapter Fifteen

"Johnny," Warren said firmly, stopping him just as he had grabbed Geoff's collar and had one fist raised. His tone of voice was commanding and the opposite of how he'd spoken in his role as butler.

"Follow me," he said without waiting for him to respond. He strode past them without even a glance and went through the door that Johnny had come through.

Johnny glared at Geoff and for a moment I thought he wouldn't let go, but he did. Interesting tactic from Warren of all people.

Everyone let out a collective sigh.

With enough swagger to intimidate even Pandora, he disappeared through the entrance.

"Damn, that was intense," Eddie muttered.

"What's interesting is that he wouldn't have done that if he had killed his wife," I said.

"Unless he wanted to make himself look innocent," Eddie said.

Miles scoffed. "That hardly made him seem innocent. I agree with Maggie. I don't think he did it."

"Even so, he might know something that can help us. Let's go." I rose to my feet. It was not like the actors were going to continue; they had all taken a break. David handed Geoff a water bottle so he could take a moment and gather himself while Brenda patted his arm.

Instead of following in Johnny's direction, we went out through the front and found a corridor with several dressing rooms and areas filled with props.

There was also a small kitchen with chairs and a table, which was also where Johnny and Warren were now seated. Their eyes briefly widened as they spotted us.

"Hi, I'm Maggie," I said, before they were inclined to throw me out. "This is Miles and this is Eddie, my associates. We, err, are looking into your wife's murder." Nothing wrong with stretching the truth a little, though Eddie would probably not appreciate being called my associate.

"Who hired you?" Johnny asked.

"Good question," I said as my brain scrambled for an answer.

"The police asked us to help," Miles said. "They don't usually do that, but we were part of the murder mystery weekend and are therefore also potential witnesses. The police are hoping we can provide invaluable insight."

Wow, he made it sound so...official.

Johnny seemed to accept it and gave a sharp nod.

Warren had his arms folded across his chest and though he appeared calm and collected, just taking a sip of his water, he also looked as if he was ready to jump up any second. Perhaps he was expecting another outburst from Valerie's lovely husband.

"I'm hoping you guys can maybe tell us a bit more about what Valerie was like. Perhaps you also have an idea about who could have done something so terrible." I sat down at the table while Eddie and Miles lingered somewhere behind me. This way it totally felt like they were my bodyguards.

"Ask those loopy plonkers on stage," Johnny said with a wave of his hand. "She spent most of her time with them, prancing around."

"You didn't approve?"

"It didn't make any money, did it? What was the point?"

"Was she friends with any of them?"

"What are you implying?" His eyes started to bulge again and it was not a good look for him.

"Well, you seemed to think one of them had killed her. Why?"

"Who else would it be? They were the only other people she spent time with."

I looked at Warren. It was still strange how he had calmed down Johnny. Then again, perhaps Johnny was just a big bully who backed down from people who knew how to handle themselves. Warren could apparently be very authoritative.

Warren sighed. "Like I was telling Johnny, I can't imagine any of them hurting Valerie."

"Who else would it be then?" Johnny raised his voice again.

"I hope we can find out," I said.

He ignored my attempt at conciliation. "She only ever spent her time here. I was glad the rehearsals had been cut to three times a week since a short while ago. Before that, she was here Monday through Friday evening."

Warren shifted her weight and looked down at the table. Aha.

"Well, thank you for your time. We won't keep you any longer." I got up and nodded to Eddie and Miles to follow me.

Behind me, I heard them say goodbye. Our footsteps were the only sound as we walked through the corridor and back to the front entrance of the theatre where I stopped.

"Okay, so rehearsals are only on Monday, Wednesday and Friday and judging by Warren's reaction he knew why Valerie had lied about that. My guess would be an affair."

"Mine too," Eddie said. "The way she had been flirting with me."

"Did she flirt with you when we weren't there as well?" I asked.

"Yeah. Sometime Saturday she came across me in the corridor and started touching my chest. She was coming on way too strong too fast. I didn't like it."

I glanced at Miles. "What about you?"

"She tried it Friday, the afternoon they arrived," he said curtly.

"But?"

"But I shut it down." His tone indicated it was as easy as flipping a switch.

"How?" Eddie and I asked.

"I told her she reminded me of my mother."

"Ouch." Eddie and I cringed at the same time.

Miles smiled as if he'd just revealed a magician's trick.

"Okay, what I'd really like to do is talk to Brenda and Geoff. All of them, really. But I'd like to start with them. I just don't want the others to be around when we do." I pressed my finger against my lip.

"Oh, I have an idea then. I still have to settle their payment. We can drop it off where they live. I can ring them tomorrow and set it up," Miles said.

"Perfect, actually. Well done. We make a pretty good team."

The front door behind me opened and I whirled around. Alistair stood there in his pristine suit. He surveyed us for a moment.

"Ah, Scooby Gang," he said.

"We're actually the Super Sleuthers." Eddie folded his arms across his chest.

"We are?" I asked him.

"I'd prefer it if we weren't," Miles said dryly.

"What? It's a good name."

"Crisis averted, actually," Miles told Alistair, and then proceeded to explain what happened.

"Hmm," Alistair said. "I'll still show my face. I think that will send the right kind of message here. Where are you heading off to now?"

We spoke all at once.

"Home," I said.

"Brian," Eddie mumbled.

"Pub," was Miles's answer.

"Alright, I might join you in the pub later." Alistair replied to Miles. He looked at me last, and then he was off. And so were we.

Christina was on the sofa watching a documentary about wildlife while Snowball had jumped onto the sofa next to her. She was currently washing her ears. Even though I had seen her do that many times, it still remained immensely adorable.

I poured myself a glass of lemonade in the kitchen and joined Christina. "What's new?" I asked.

"Did you hear that Pandora viciously attacked one of Emblyn's friends? Okay, not really viciously attacked, he got pecked on the ankle a few times."

"Really? Was it this Elijah bloke?" I asked, fighting the urge to roll my eyes. What was it about this guy?

"I'm not sure, Dawn mentioned it when she delivered the post."

"She must have noticed something off about him," I said.

Christina drew her eyes away from the TV. "It sounds as if you don't like him. Why?"

"I don't know. I only met him once but he immediately brought out my protective instincts." I shrugged. "I should probably cut him some slack. I don't even know him."

"Mags, hate to break it to you, but intuition is a powerful ally."

I bit my lip. "That is true."

"Any news about the murder?"

"We think she might have been having an affair, but we don't know if that's true, nor with whom if it is."

"Interesting. And you still don't know why she was outside at midnight?"

I shook my head. "If it was to talk with someone from the murder mystery weekend, I don't see why they'd be outside. But then again, why would someone else drive up to the Pembroke and meet with her at midnight?"

"Do you think she was up to something? Like, maybe she was planning on robbing Miles." Christina had a glint in her eyes.

"Apparently I'm rubbing off on you. You do realise that that's very unlikely and we have no proof for that?"

"Ha. And apparently Alistair is rubbing off on you."

"If only," Detective Black sighed.

"Don't worry, I'm keeping an open mind. So far, all we know is that she likes to flirt and that until recently she was gone most evenings." I tapped my finger against my lips. "You know, she could have just stepped outside to get some fresh air. Maybe someone in the Pembroke saw her and followed her outside."

"Do you think the killer intended to go out and kill her? Or was it to talk to her and then it ended up in murder?"

"Too soon to tell. But I heard voices and they didn't sound upset or anything, so my guess is they were discussing something. It doesn't necessarily mean a fight erupted, it could be that the killer didn't like whatever was being discussed and decided to end it there and then."

"Eddie said she was killed with your scarf."

I shivered. "Yeah."

"I'm sorry."

"We'll find out who did it. Besides, there's plenty of good things going on in our lives. Our other flatmate is a cute, fluffy bunny, you're dating someone, I'm...working on a novel."

Christina raised an eyebrow. "You're always working on a novel."

"Not always. Right now I'm watching a documentary about—" I looked up just in time to see two rhinos mate.

"Great," I muttered while Christina laughed.

Chapter Sixteen

The next day at two o'clock in the afternoon, Miles rang my doorbell. He held open the door to his BMW for me.

"Look at you being a gentleman," I said.

"I guess I have my moments." He shut the door and got back behind the wheel.

"Hello," Eddie's voice said close to my ear, making me yelp.

He chuckled. "Surprised you, did I?"

I looked over my shoulder. "I wasn't sure if you would join us on your day off."

"I'm part of the Super Sleuthers, remember?"

"You really think we need a collective name, do you?" I asked.

Miles finished typing the address in his Sat Nav and smirked at me before driving off.

"And next you'll want us to come up with a battle cry and an intricate hand shake." I shook my head.

"Yes! Let's do that too."

BRENDA AND GEOFF'S home was a detached property with a white picket fence, a white bench in the front garden, and a wooden door at the side of the house that led to the back garden. It looked well kept and was spacious enough. Brenda was a librarian and Geoff an accountant. I wasn't sure how much they made, but it looked like they had plenty of money.

Miles had called ahead like he'd said he would, so they were expecting us and opened the door before Miles could even ring the doorbell.

The plan was for Miles to take the lead; we wanted it to appear we were simply in the neighbourhood and wanted to take care of the payment. Geoff had declined the offer of the second half of the payment since we hadn't really gotten our money's worth, but Miles had convinced him to accept it; he genuinely wanted to pay them.

Geoff was the one who opened the door and led us to the reception room. The hallway and the room itself were very clean and tidy. There was some art work on the walls and the sofa and flat screen were some of the first things I noticed. There was also a large piano in the corner.

"The piano is new," Geoff said as he saw me study it. "Isn't she a beauty?"

Detective Black sighed. "I don't trust people who refer to inanimate objects as 'she,'" he said. "Next, he'll try to have a conversation with the toaster."

As opposed to a made-up person in someone's head?

"How dare you call me made-up," Detective Black said as he glared at me.

"Do you play?" I asked Geoff.

"No, but I'd like to. Some day."

I frowned. He made it sound as if he had bought the piano on a whim. Who would do that?

"Please sit." Geoff himself sat down in a leather armchair while us Super Sleuthers took place on the cream-coloured sofa.

Brenda tottered in with a tray containing a tea pot, cups, milk and sugar, and biscuits.

Damn it. The temptation of biscuits was too much. At least I'd managed to snack once a week for a few weeks. And I had *looked* at yoga studios so there was that. Yes, I could indulge a little. After all, this was a murder investigation. Biscuits were a part of that.

"So nice to see you again. It was dreadful to part in such circumstances," Brenda said with a smile. "Tea?"

"Yes, please," we all murmured.

What English person declines tea?

She poured for us but left us to add milk or sugar ourselves. Eddie always dowsed his tea in sugar and Miles took it black. I added a bit of sugar and a bit of milk.

"You can tell a lot by how someone takes their tea," Detective Black said.

I blinked at him, waiting for him to say more but he simply smiled at me.

"How are you both doing?" Miles asked. "Were you close with Valerie?"

Brenda's eyebrow shot up but she brought it back down again and gave a surreptitious glance at her husband. He had responded to the question by puffing out his cheeks and then nodding gravely.

"She was a lovely girl," Brenda said without the emotions that should accompany those words.

"Good actress, too," Geoff said.

That was my opening. "Yes, she's had a lot of leading roles, from what I saw on your website." I smiled and took a sip of my tea, trying not to look too eager about what would come out of his mouth next. I did observe Brenda stiffening from the corner of my eye.

"Yes, that's right. She loved acting." He looked as if he wanted to say more but wasn't sure what.

Eddie slurped his tea. "That's good tea," he said.

Brenda gave him a genuine smile. "Thank you, dear."

"Had she been looking forward to the performance this weekend?" I asked. "I mean, since she was going to be the victim." It wasn't exactly a leading role.

"Oh, yes, quite. She actually requested the role of the victim," Geoff said. "Not sure why, but she wanted to."

"Had you ever done a performance like this before?" Miles asked.

"No. We were all quite excited." He sagged a little, like a balloon letting out air. "It didn't go at all as expected."

Detective Black scoffed. "Understatement of the year."

"Well, we would still like to pay for your efforts. I'm sure it would have been incredible," Miles said in a gentle tone.

Geoff immediately perked up. "Yes, yes. I think you would have loved it, you know?" He went on about all the things he had planned which was interesting and I wanted to know more, but this was my chance to snoop.

"May I use your restroom?" I asked Brenda.

"Of course. Follow me."

I shot a glance at Eddie, hoping he would catch my meaning. He would have to keep her preoccupied so I could nose around.

She moved halfway through the hallway before pointing at a door. "There you go."

Thanks." I looked at her to give her a smile, but my eyes were drawn to the pictures on the wall behind her. There were a lot of them, and all of them were pictures of her and her husband. A wedding picture from many years ago, a picture in front of the Eiffel Tower, one in a pub. Some looked more recent and in others Geoff's hair was darker and fuller and Brenda had longer hair than now, or sometimes shorter.

But I also noticed something missing.

"You don't have kids?"

There was a flattening of the lips before she turned them upwards in a cold smile. "No. We were not blessed."

"I'm so sorry," I said, meaning it. "That must have been very difficult, but you do seem so happy with each other."

Behind her dark eyes was a flash of genuine emotion though I couldn't be sure what it was. Affection?

"Yes, we are. He's the love of my life. Always has been and always will be."

I touched her arm. "That's so beautiful. And that itself is a blessing. Not everyone has that kind of love."

She tilted her head ever so slightly and then placed her hand over mine. "Thank you."

I made my way to the bathroom. Since it was a downstairs one, I had expected a simple toilet and sink in a cramped room, but I was wrong. It really was an actual bathroom with a shower and bath, a towel rack and scented candles and not one, but two sinks. I had never before realised that one sink wasn't enough. Now I desperately wanted two as well.

Detective Black rolled his eyes. "Really? Who's going to join you while you're brushing your teeth? Apart from me."

"It could happen," I whispered.

"And then you'd be brushing your teeth at the same time? Every night? I doubt that."

There were no cabinets above the sinks, so I unlocked the door and peered out into the hallway. She had gone back to the reception room.

"What exactly are we looking for?" Detective Black asked.

"This place has got to have a study," I said. "That's where all the paperwork will be and hopefully any stuff related to The Dramateers. I can't help but feel that it's important somehow. I mean, why else was she killed during this weekend?" I tried a door opposite the bathroom and found it unlocked.

It really was the only other downstairs room apart from the one directly opposite the reception room, but I couldn't go there now, since Brenda would see me.

"Bingo," I said as I stared at the desk with a computer and lots of papers. I slipped inside and closed the door behind me.

"A diary, here," Detective Black said as he pointed.

I opened it to today. There was nothing there, so I went back to Friday. Geoff had written 'Pembroke' down and the rest of the days were blank. I flicked through the earlier days and weeks, seeing if I could find anything that could be remotely suspicious.

"There," Detective Black pointed.

And that's when Eddie's voice—higher than usual—and Brenda's sounded in the hallway.

Chapter Seventeen

I shut the diary and crept to the door to listen closely. I pressed my ear to the wood and heard them both pass me by. They had gone into the kitchen. Eddie sounded less panicked, probably because Brenda hadn't noticed that the bathroom was no longer occupied, and this was my cue to get out. I slowly opened the door. The kitchen was large enough that I could leave the office without her directly spotting me.

I slipped out and shut the door quietly while I heard Eddie still chatting away. I glanced back but they were both out of my line of sight. It meant that I wasn't in theirs either.

When I returned to the reception room, Geoff and Miles were laughing about something. I sat back down next to Miles and waited to see if I had caught them in the middle of a conversation. I hadn't.

"What did you do again, Geoff? Apart from running The Dramateers," I said.

"I'm an accountant," he said. "Boring, I know. But I like it well enough."

"Do you have an office then or do you work from home?"

"I have several clients. I usually meet them."

"Ah, I see. That must be annoying. Or do you get to meet up at fancy hotels where they pay for your lunch?" I chuckled.

"Nothing fancy, no. I meet them at their place of business or at home. Say," he said as he leaned forward at the same time that Eddie and Brenda returned with a fresh pot of tea. Eddie looked relieved at the sight of me. "I read an article about you helping out with a murder in Castlefield."

It meant he had been checking me out. It wasn't a recent article.

"Yes, that's right," I said. "But the papers were definitely exaggerating."

"Still, it's impressive. Do you think you'll help the police with Valerie's death?" I couldn't tell if he would want me to say yes or no. I glanced at Brenda whose expression was unreadable. There was tension in her shoulders, yes, but it had been there the entire time. Even out in the hallway when it was just the two of us.

"I am sure the police will solve her murder quickly," I said, not really answering.

I think they both realised that.

"Well," Miles said. "We should be going." He handed Geoff an envelope.

"You really don't have to do this, but I appreciate it. You're a man of honour."

Eddie coughed, probably stifling a laugh.

"Thank you," Miles said politely.

"Before you go, Maggie, why don't you follow me and I'll give you a leaflet for the next performance." Brenda didn't wait for my reply and left the room. I exchanged glances with Miles and Eddie and hurried after her.

She went into the study where she handed me a piece of paper with the title *Worse for Wear* and a black and white picture of Brenda tearing off her own dress—not that it revealed anything inappropriate. It was a very artful image. And as I scanned the other names, Valerie's wasn't on there.

"Damn," Detective Black said. "They didn't wait long to print a new flyer for the play."

"Valerie isn't as nice and innocent as Geoff makes her sound," Brenda said quietly. "She was having it on with David. She even said—well, she told me she was pregnant and didn't know if it was David's or Johnny's."

My mouth opened. What? No, wait. That wasn't possible.

"Alistair would have mentioned it," Detective Black said. "They've already done the autopsy."

"I see," I said. It meant that either Brenda was lying or Valerie had.

ALISTAIR HAD ARRIVED at the Rose before we did. He was dressed in a nice shirt and dark trousers. His blazer was placed over the back of the chair.

I smiled when our eyes met and he winked at me.

"Solved the murder already?" he asked with a grin.

He seemed awfully relaxed about my investigative outing, but I figured that had to do with the fact that Eddie and Miles had been with me today.

I sat down opposite Alistair while Miles sat next to me and Eddie plopped down across from him.

"We may not have solved the murder, but we do come bearing clues," I said.

We ordered tea and lunch. I had a sandwich with goat's cheese and walnuts.

"Valerie wasn't pregnant, was she?" I asked Alistair.

All three men looked at me in surprise.

"No. She wasn't pregnant," Alistair said. "Why do you ask?"

"Because Brenda said that Valerie had told her she was. And that she wasn't sure if it belonged to her husband or to…David."

I was hoping for a dramatic gasp or two, but Miles simply raised an eyebrow, Eddie was consuming his turkey sandwich with vigour, and Alistair's lips twitched ever so slightly.

"Maybe she only thought she was pregnant," Alistair said. "But she could have been having an affair. There was no evidence of that on her phone, but it wouldn't hurt to talk to David."

While I was chewing, Miles took it upon himself to fill him in on the rest. "Maggie also found Geoff's diary and a few times in the space of a couple of weeks, he had an appointment at a hotel called The Golden Goose. Since he says he doesn't meet clients in hotels, it might mean he's having an affair. At least, that's what Maggie thinks. I'm not sure he would write such visits down in his diary, but people have done worse ill-advised things."

"You can say that again," Alistair said. "Okay, anything else?"

"Brenda was clearly jealous of Valerie and the fact that she was a leading lady all the time. She now has the main role in the next play. They've already printed a new leaflet. It included a professional picture of Brenda. How she had that made so quickly…" I said.

Alistair sat back. "Wow. That is very odd. She's either very callous or she knew Valerie wouldn't be in the play."

"I think that might be something you want to ask Brenda about when you speak with her. I mean, you are going to speak with her, right?" I asked.

"I will first look into Geoff and who he was meeting at the hotel. If he was having an affair with Valerie, then I'll have more ammo when I go talk to them. If I can't find anything, I can just pay them a visit and ask them a few more basic questions about what kind of person Valerie was and then mention the leaflet."

"They also seem to have a lot of money. I don't know how much being an accountant and librarian earns, of course, but still."

"Could be an inheritance," Miles said as he picked out a piece of cucumber and moved it to the side of his plate.

"They don't have any kids," I said. "So that probably helped them save money. I forgot to ask him, though, how he finances the plays and everything. I mean—he's created The Dramateers and I think he rents the theatre where they perform each month. That must still cost a pretty penny, right? Not to mention that piano he bought on a whim."

"Also something I can ask and look into," Alistair said.

"Good. So the...Super Sleuthers did well?" I asked.

Despite the fact that Eddie had his face buried deep within the core of his sandwich, he looked up with a glint in his eyes.

"You're really sticking with that name, then?" Alistair asked with a frown.

He was totally judging the name. I couldn't blame him.

Eddie frowned at Alistair. "Yes. What's wrong with it? It has alli—alligatoration." He glanced at me.

"Alliteration. Yes. And it sums up what we are perfectly."

"I can't believe you're defending that name," Miles said with a chuckle.

"Regardless of any kind of name, you did well." Alistair nodded at me.

I felt surprisingly good at the sound of him complimenting me.

"Don't beam too much," Detective Black said, "or you'll blind everyone in this room."

But I was disappointed that I couldn't be there when Alistair questioned them. I wanted to contribute and I wanted to see things through. Instead, DC Daniels had that honour.

Then again, it was probably safer this way. I was definitely eager to help and slightly addicted to solving mysteries, but I myself didn't want any repeat of what happened last time. Or the time before that.

The thing about murderers, I realised, was that they were entirely too murdery.

"Well said," Detective Black said dryly.

AFTER LUNCH, WE ALL walked back around to the village square where we would all scatter back to wherever we were supposed to be. We passed Put A Ring On It, our local jewellery shop. Carry, paler than when I last saw her, was looking up at the shop and occasionally snapped a picture with her smartphone. The front window was broken.

"Carry, how are you?" Alistair asked. "I heard about the robbery."

"What? There was a robbery?" I said with an open mouth. There was plenty of crime in Castlefield, but most of it involved runaway sheep or teens trying to buy alcohol, and save for the occasional murder, nothing much happened. Of course, we did have our very own crime boss: Pandora. Quite literally from the underworld.

Our morning outing meant that the three of us had missed that particular piece of gossip.

"Was anyone hurt?" Eddie asked. We didn't know Carry that well, but well enough.

"No, no." She waved a dismissive hand. "It happened last night. I'm insured, so I suppose it's not too bad. It's just that, well, I don't like the thought of something like that being able to happen here. This is my home and I've always felt safe. Now I suddenly feel quite paranoid." She glanced over her shoulder as if to prove her point.

"I'm so sorry, Carry. I assure you the police are doing their best to look into it," Alistair said in a soothing voice. He was quite good at that; even I felt reassured.

She smiled a toothy smile. "Thanks, officer. I feel much better knowing you're around."

Alistair nodded politely and we continued on our way. We stopped near The Wicked Bookworm and said our goodbyes. Miles decided to take a stroll through the village with Eddie—they really were becoming good friends—and Alistair went on home.

I went straight to Nancy's shop where Emblyn was working. She was at the counter and her eyes widened when she spotted me.

"Hello, Emblyn," I said in a cheery tone.

"Maggie, hi. I'm so excited for tonight. I've already got snacks." The excitement she described didn't match her tone.

"What's wrong? You don't sound happy."

She smiled weakly. "Of course I am."

"Does it have to do with Elijah?" I narrowed my eyes at her, hoping she wouldn't lie to me. I would be able to tell.

She frowned. "Of course not. Why are you asking me about that? Not everybody has issues, you know? And not everything is a mystery."

"Defensiveness," I said slowly, "is a sign of lying."

She scrunched up her nose and looked away.

"Everything is fine," she said.

"Then why aren't you smiling? You always smile and make jokes and you ask me about the 'hot detective' and you would want to know more about the murder. You're upset and you can tell me what it is. I won't judge you." I would judge Elijah, though, if he did indeed have something to do with this. Actually, I'd more than judge him.

She looked down at her hands again. "It's fine. He's just—I saw him talking with another girl. Maybe he likes her better."

"Talking or flirting?"

She shrugged.

In my mind I was already going through the potential weapons I could use on him. A ladle? A chair? An ironing board? What if I tied him to a tree and summoned Pandora? But I decided to take the mature approach.

"It could have meant nothing. Just because it was a girl he was talking with, doesn't mean he likes her that way. If you feel really insecure about it, you can always ask him."

Her eyes widened. "No way. Then he'll think I'm psycho jealous."

I rolled my eyes. "I'm sure he won't. Communication is very important in any kind of relationship. However, if you don't want to outright ask him, you can always just casually ask him about that girl and see how he reacts."

She pursed her lips.

"It appears she likes the sneaky approach," Detective Black said with a hint of judgy-ness.

"Don't worry. I'm sure it's fine. If he really likes you, you'll know." I smiled at her.

She managed a smile back.

I couldn't help but be very thankful that my angst-ridden teenage years were behind me.

"Yes. Now you just have angst-ridden adult years," Detective Black said with a smirk.

Chapter Eighteen

Emblyn wouldn't show up until seven thirty that evening, so I had dinner with Christina and worked on the final rounds of edits before sending the book to my editor. It meant that I could focus on this murder for a while.

I had some time to spare, so I decided to knit on the sofa while the gentle tapping of raindrops on the window functioned as background noise. I really loved autumn. Of course, it also meant that it was likely I was about to venture out into the rain, but that was why people had invented umbrellas.

At exactly seven thirty, the bell rang and I opened the door. It was still raining and Alistair was holding a black umbrella.

"Alistair, hi," I said, processing the fact that he was not Emblyn.

"A little birdy mentioned some sort of Stanley stake-out." I could tell he was struggling to keep from smiling.

"You make it sound more exciting than what it is." I stepped aside to let him in.

"Emblyn is supposed to be here. Did you see her on your way over?"

"No, sorry. I hope you don't mind if I tag along. I'm sure you'll not encounter anything dangerous, but you know, Pandora is out there."

I winced. "Good point. And no, it's actually a good thing that you're here. The reason I invited Emblyn over is so that maybe I can get her to open up about this new guy that's hanging around her. I don't trust him."

He frowned. "Who and why not?"

I told him about Elijah and what I'd overheard.

"It could be something, but it could also be harmless teenage stuff."

"She doesn't really have parents to talk to, so I am hoping she'll open up to me. I mean, she likes mysteries and excitement and though I'm sure Stanley isn't up to anything nefarious, there's a possibility this will be a nice bonding moment for her and me."

He had quirked his eyebrow at the word 'nefarious' but was back to his neutral detective-mode expression. He was always so hard to read when he was like that. Despite the fact that we were friends, it still didn't feel as if he completely let his guard down around me. Or anyone else. But we had come a long way, and every time I saw a bit more of the real Alistair, I felt closer to him.

"Of course," he said politely.

"Let's wait outside Stanley and Olivia's cottage while I text Emblyn." I pulled open the door and we stepped outside. It was still raining and Alistair used his umbrella to protect us both, though his left shoulder was still getting wet.

"We should take my car, though. You don't know where he's going; it could be far."

"I was going to take Nancy's car, but okay. We can take yours."

We stepped into his black VW Beetle that I had a crush on. Then again, Nancy's Land Rover was also very nice. Old, but nice.

Alistair was quiet as I sent a message to Emblyn. She responded after a few seconds saying she couldn't make it.

I scoffed.

"What?" Alistair asked.

"She just texted back that she can't make it. Why didn't she let me know sooner? This doesn't seem like her. You don't think she's in trouble, do you?"

"Of course not. You're forgetting she's a teen."

"Okay, Mr Cynical. She was excited about tonight and even said she'd bring snacks."

"But you said a boy was involved. If romance is in the air, all bets are off." Alistair shrugged. "Trust me."

"Is that what you were like when you were a teen? You'd ditch your friends for a pretty girl?"

He grinned. "Definitely. Sadly, I never got that opportunity."

"What? You were so popular. On Valentine's Day you'd always get a heap of roses."

"Never from the girl I like," he said with a quick glance at me, but then his eyes were on the road. It took us two minutes to arrive at Stanley's cottage.

"He's talking about you," Detective Black said from the back seat.

It's not like he needed to say that. I remembered his confession a while ago.

"He also said 'like' and not 'liked,' Detective Black said.

I felt a flutter of something in my chest.

Alistair parked his car on the opposite side of the cobbled street. We weren't directly in front of the cottage, but we still had a visual.

"I really wish we had snacks," I said after four seconds.

Alistair's chuckle was soft. "Check the glove compartment."

I gasped in excitement and opened it. "Yes." I clapped in joy, then took out the bag of salty crisps and checked out the variety of sweets he had in there. "I think we should get married."

He laughed. "If I had known that was going to be your response, I would have done it sooner."

"Definitely. Food is the way to my heart." I opened a bag of Skittles.

Alistair watched me eat a handful of Skittles, then turned his attention to the cottage. The lights were on and their white van was parked at the side of the cottage.

"So did you have a nice meal with Miles?" he asked without looking at me.

There was no tone to be detected, but I still got the impression that maybe he asked because he was jealous. Not that he had anything to worry about.

"You sure?" Detective Black asked.

I turned around and glared at him. Alistair didn't notice.

"Yes, it was quite nice. Did you have a nice dinner as well?"

"I just had a quick sandwich instead of a warm meal. I was busy checking out the crime scene again and going over the case so far."

"Any news?"

"Nothing we didn't already know. She died from asphyxiation and she was definitely killed with yo—a scarf. From behind. It could have been done by a man or woman. I also spoke with Brenda and Geoff again. Geoff didn't seem to know that

Valerie had told Brenda about being pregnant. Brenda swore she had no idea why she'd said that and seemed shocked when I told her she hadn't been pregnant."

"What if Valerie said it to mess with Brenda?"

"Why do you say that?" Alistair asked.

"Because Brenda and Geoff couldn't have kids. Maybe she did it out of spite. To rub it in that she could have kids—well, pretend like she could—in order to make Brenda envious."

"That would give Brenda a motive."

"Yeah. But I'd definitely heard a man and woman talking. I mean, technically, there could have been more people, but it's likely it was Valerie and the man who killed her."

"Right," Alistair said. "I'm more suspicious about the husband. We don't have proof yet, but there's something off about him."

I nodded. "He does seem to have a temper. I hope it's not him, though. Imagine the person you're supposed to love and trust the most would do something like that."

Alistair placed his hand on mine and squeezed. "I know. That's why I get very obsessed with a case. I can't stand the idea of someone getting away with taking someone else's life. It doesn't bring back the person, but at least the murderer is punished and can't hurt anyone else when they're caught."

"Then it's a good thing you're joining me on this case, which will probably turn out to be nothing." I hoped. Otherwise I really was going to lose my faith in humanity. Stanley was one of the sweetest men I knew.

"Show time," Alistair said as Stanley came out of the house and started walking down the street.

"He's not taking his car," I said.

"Okay, then neither are we. Let's go." Alistair was already out of the car before I could respond. I took my Skittles with me.

Alistair held the umbrella, and to protect us from the rain, I had to press myself up against him.

"Yeah, right," Detective Black scoffed.

We followed at a safe distance. Far enough so he wouldn't recognise our faces, but close enough that we could see where he was going.

"We should hold hands," I said.

"What?"

"If he does look back, he'll think we're a couple and dismiss us. He wouldn't look any closer or question why we are out walking."

Alistair paused for so long that I thought he was going to dismiss it, especially since the umbrella already hid our features and we were already walking close together. But then I felt his cold hand around mine.

Play it cool, Maggie. Definitely don't grin like an idiot or make happy noises.

Stanley walked briskly along in the direction of the church. My first thought was that he was going into the woods, which immediately cranked up the creepy factor, but instead he went into the church. We stopped on the corner as we watched him go in.

"Why would he go into the church? Do you think he's having an affair with someone at the church? Isn't that blasphemy?" I asked.

"You think that's blasphemy? What about the murder that happened last summer?"

"Also blasphemy."

A woman walked up to the church and headed in.

I gasped. "Eleanor is going to beat the crap out of Stanley. And so is Olivia. Actually, all the women from the book club will. Hell, I will even join in."

Alistair squeezed my hand. "Let's go check it out."

I grunted. "I'm not sure we should go in. What if they're naked?"

"I don't think they're doing what you think they're doing. I mean, why go to the church? Why not a hotel or somewhere else?"

Alistair pulled me along towards the church.

"Where exactly? The Pembroke is no longer a hotel and the local B&B isn't exactly the spot for a secret affair. If she's married as well, they won't be able to go to her place, so...you know, a church actually makes sense."

Alistair stopped by the church's gate and turned to me. We were still holding hands. "You make a good point."

I waved my other arm. "I know!"

"Still. We will look and get the proof so that he can't deny it and then he can break the news to Olivia himself."

I let out a little whine at the thought. Poor Olivia. She'd already been through so much with that scumbag of a first husband.

Alistair petted my head. "Don't worry. It will be okay."

We walked up to the church and opened the door. Alistair went in first and I followed.

It took us a moment to process what we were seeing and then I screamed.

Chapter Nineteen

"Argh, my eyes!" I slapped my hands in front of them so I could block out what I'd seen. Would it be bad if I used bleach to scrub out my brain?

Alistair coughed as if he didn't know quite what to say. "Terribly sorry for the disturbance. My friend did not mean to scream."

I nodded. "I did."

"We will leave you in peace. Excuse us."

He ushered me out of the church and shut the creaking door. Then we looked at each other, both of us carrying expressions of horror and then we started laughing. It started with a chuckle, but then it ended up as a full-blown, slightly hysterical laugh.

"W—we should go," Alistair said in between laughter. "Before they think we're laughing at them."

I laughed too hard to be able to respond. Again, Alistair grabbed my hand and pulled me along. By the time we got to the bridge near my flat, we had stopped laughing. My stomach was sore and I was drying the tears that had streamed down my face.

"I can't believe the things you drag me into," Alistair said in an amused tone.

"It would be so boring otherwise, wouldn't it?"

"Quite." He smiled at me.

"Wow, him being a nude model for an art class was not even near the realm of possibilities for me. You know, I don't think I can ever eat a piece of fruit again."

Alistair chuckled. "It wasn't that bad, was it?"

We both contemplated this.

"It was," we said simultaneously and laughed.

"So what is your next step in this case of yours?"

"I'm just going to tell Olivia he's not cheating on her and that she should ask him. I'm sure she wouldn't actually mind. I mean, it is kind of a good thing he's doing, right? It's just that I hadn't expected it at all."

"No, neither had I. Though we had predicted nudity, so that's at least one thing we got right."

"Yes, but I never saw this coming. Then again, I didn't think he would cheat on Olivia either. He dotes on her."

"You never know."

"Don't say that."

"Okay." He smiled.

"I'm sure you see a lot of bad stuff, but there is also plenty of good in this world."

Alistair bit his bottom lip. "True. It would just be naive to think that people aren't capable of making mistakes."

"Oh, I know people make mistakes. But not everyone will make the same ones. Not everyone is a cheater or a killer. Besides, a person is not their mistakes."

He raised his eyebrows and looked at me with surprise. "Huh. I guess...I guess that's true. I like that." His smile was slow and sweet.

I felt my cheeks warm. "Anyway. I've got it from here. I'll see you around." Before I could respond, I gave him a little wave and darted off to my flat. When I looked back at him, he was standing on the bridge with his arm spread and his eyes closed as the wind ruffled his hair.

"Ha. You're rubbing off on him," Detective Black said. "Before you know it, he'll be as weird as you are."

"I hope not." I kind of liked him just as he was.

WEDNESDAY MORNING I got up on time. First, to phone Olivia and tell her about Stanley. Second, to help out in The Wicked Bookworm. Both Christina and Eddie were working and they didn't really need my help, but I wanted to keep busy while I contemplated the recent murder.

"Funnily enough I do my best brainstorming in the shower or on the toilet," Detective Black said.

I wrinkled my nose as I was in the back, rearranging the children's books. "If you don't mind, I'm not going to write about that."

"Of course not," he huffed. "I would like *some* privacy."

I smiled.

"Ah, there you are," a familiar voice said.

I turned to see Alistair. His hair was damp as if he'd just showered and a spicy scent reached my nose. A new aftershave?

"I just wanted you to know I did some digging on the husband. I was lucky because there wasn't an actual file since nobody ended up being charged, but I found out that Johnny Cooke and Warren Lowe got into a physical altercation about a month ago."

My eyes widened. "Johnny and Warren? Have to say, that surprises me. Not about Johnny, but Warren seems so calm. Although that could be because I know him in his role as the butler."

Alistair raised an eyebrow. "I looked into Warren and found out he was dishonourably discharged from the army."

I blinked. "Wow, you really are a source of information. This is very good."

Alistair flashed me a charming smile as his cheeks coloured. "Just doing my job."

"Are you going to talk to Johnny and Warren next?"

"Yes, I'm going with DC Daniels."

I was disappointed I couldn't go with him. I had enjoyed teaming up with Alistair the last time there was a murder, but he already had a partner. "Thanks for letting me know. That's very sweet of you."

"You're welcome. What are your plans for the day?"

"I'm going to be working here and hope that my subconscious can solve this murder." I grinned at him.

"That would be great. I'll see you later today." To my surprise he leaned forward and kissed me on the cheek.

I watched him leave, a warm and fuzzy feeling settle in my chest.

"Don't say it," I said to Detective Black.

He made a gesture as if to zip his lips.

Things were quiet enough in the shop during the morning, which meant that I had time to visit Emblyn and see why she stood me up yesterday. Right before lunch time I slipped through the curtain and made my way into Nancy's shop.

Nancy herself was behind the counter, ringing up a customer. I gave her a quick kiss and then made my way over to Emblyn who was over at the incense, sprucing up the display with the statues of deities and different-shaped candles. She turned and smiled as she sensed someone approaching, but her smile faltered when she realised it was me.

"Hi," I said.

"Oh, hi." Her tone was less enthusiastic than mine.

"Care to explain why you ditched me last night? I thought you were excited about it."

She pouted. "I'm sorry. I shouldn't have done that."

I studied her face. Apart from the pouting, she didn't look remotely upset. "You're not upset at all. What happened? Did Elijah ask you to be his girlfriend?" I folded my arms and raised an eyebrow.

Her pout transformed into a smile. "No, but we kissed." Her eyes glittered.

"Was it your first kiss?"

"No," she said defensively and looked down. "Okay, yes."

"There's no time limit on when you should be kissed, you know? I was eighteen when I had my first kiss."

"Really?"

"Yep. Now, dish." I managed a smile. To be honest, I was just happy that she was happy and I realised that I had been overprotective when it concerned Elijah. I didn't even know the bloke.

"It was very sweet. He gave me this beautiful necklace." She pulled out a golden chain with a white, glittering stone at the bottom. I had absolutely no idea if it was a diamond or anything else.

The necklace looked incredibly expensive. My mind immediately went to the robbery, though I doubted that if Elijah had anything to do with that, he'd be stupid enough to give a stolen item to someone else to show in public.

"Where did he get that? It's beautiful." I tried to sound as normal as possible.

Emblyn beamed. "No idea. It is, though. Isn't it?"

I nodded. "So things are going well? Are you dating?"

She waved a dismissive hand. "Labels aren't cool anymore. But yeah, things are going well."

The part about the labels sounded more as if it was coming from someone else. Emblyn was more of a romantic than that.

"Just as long as you stay true to yourself," I said.

"Why wouldn't I?" That defensive tone was back again and her shoulders tensed.

I shrugged. "Just a general tip. And know that you can always talk to me about anything. I mean it."

Her shoulders relaxed and she nodded. "Okay, thanks. I appreciate that. And I'm really sorry I missed last night. Did you find out if Steve was cheating?"

"It's Stanley. And no, he wasn't cheating."

Her eyes widened. "Oops. I went and got a muffin this morning and called him Steve."

I chuckled. "It's okay. He is not easily offended. Just call him Stanley next time and all is forgiven."

She smiled sheepishly. "Good."

"Now, excuse me. I have an errand to run. See you later."

"Bye."

I waved at Nancy who was still chatting with the woman who had bought a meditation cushion. She waved back.

I was wearing a warm pullover and didn't want to go back upstairs to fetch my coat, so I left the shop and walked down the street, straight to Put a Ring on It. Carry was behind the counter and the glass that had previously been broken was now fixed.

"Wow, the windows were fixed quickly," I said by way of greeting. "That's a relief."

She looked me up and down. "Yes, it really is."

"How are you holding up?" I smiled at her. Despite the Bakery Incident, I was sure we could be pleasant.

She sighed. "I guess I'm okay. I just—I never thought something like this would happen."

"I'm sorry. At least it didn't happen while you were here."

"I wish it had! I would have given those punks a run for their money."

She suddenly reminded me of my aunt and I couldn't help but smile even wider. "I don't doubt for one second that you would have."

At that she seemed pleased, and she nodded at me. "Is there anything else I can help you with, dear? Or did you just stop to check on me?"

"I know this may be an odd request, but is there any way I can see what was stolen?"

She frowned. "You want to know what was taken? Are you investigating this too?"

Oh, great. Of course the whole village knew I was looking into the murder as well. My reputation really was preceding me.

"I'm interested in this case, yes," I said.

"I have a whole list, but I gave it to the police and the insurance company. It was a copy, though. I have a binder in the back. Let me grab it for you." She hurried away into the back of the jewellery shop and I waited patiently until she returned.

"Here you go." She flipped open the folder and went through it, pointing out all the things that had been taken from their display cases. It was quite a lot.

None of the items she pointed out to me matched the necklace that I had seen on Emblyn's neck. I was actually quite relieved.

Apparently, I saw crime everywhere.

"Occupational hazard," Detective Black said. "I once suspected my neighbour of being a drugs dealer when in reality she was hosting nudity parties in her back garden."

Of course.

Chapter Twenty

I made it back to my bookshop when my mobile phone went off. The display told me it wasn't someone I knew. I never liked it when I didn't know who was calling, but I decided to answer.

"Maggie Matthews," I said.

"Err, hello. It's David." He sounded hesitant.

My heart beat a little faster. Wouldn't it be handy if he rang to say he was the killer? It would save me a lot of bother.

"Admit it," Detective Black said. "You like the bother."

"I'm sorry to ring you, but I understand that you're looking into Valerie's death and I was just wondering if—well, I may have some information. I just—well, I'm just not comfortable telling the police. Not that I did anything—I'm sorry, I'm not explaining this well."

I bit my lip. "Why don't we talk somewhere." *Somewhere public.*

"Do you want to meet up at my local pub? It's called The Drunk Cow, not hard to find."

"Sure. I can be there in twenty minutes."

"Okay, see you then." He hung up.

"I'm not sure if this is a good sign or a bad sign," I said to Detective Black. "Maybe he's planning something."

I bit my lip. He wouldn't have suggested the pub if he was plotting my demise, and I had the feeling I'd get more out of him if I came on my own. It was very likely he didn't see me as a threat.

"Ha. He doesn't know you then." Detective Black grinned at me.

I grinned back.

I BORROWED NANCY'S Land Rover, which was parked out back, but decided to call Miles at the last minute. It was a moment of weakness, but fate had apparently already decided I was to go on my own because Miles didn't pick up.

"I guess Super Sleuthers has to be Super Sleuth for now." I started the car and drove towards Woolfield.

When I arrived, I no longer felt nervous. Instead, excitement bubbled to the surface. Perhaps I should have become a detective; it seemed I enjoyed solving murders way too much.

"It's never too late," Detective Black said helpfully.

David was in the back of the pub and had already ordered an iced tea for himself. He smiled when he saw me and I smiled back. I hadn't really expected him to be so polite considering why I was here. Then again, perhaps he was grateful that I was looking into the murder. Perhaps he had really loved her and wanted the killer caught as much as I did.

One could only hope.

"Helpful suspects are the best suspects," Detective Black said and lingered near my back.

"How are you doing?" I asked.

He ran a hand through his hair. "It still hasn't hit me yet. I keep expecting her to pop up and yell surprise. It just doesn't seem like it's possible. She was so full of life and she—" he choked.

"I'm sorry for your loss. I really mean that. I know you cared about her a lot."

"You do?" he looked up, frowning.

"Yes. It's clear from all the pictures on The Dramateers website." I didn't want to point the finger to Brenda just yet. Nor did I want to ask the questions burning on my tongue. He had invited me. I would wait to see what he would tell me.

His mouth opened like a gaping fish, then he closed it again and sighed. "The thing is, we had been having an affair for about three months, but I ended things last week."

I nodded. "I see. Do you have proof that you broke things off?" I asked, feeling more and more like a detective.

"Err, I don't know. No, wait, I do! I have a few text messages that I took screenshots of."

"Good. Keep them. How did she take the break-up?"

"Not well. She didn't like that I was the one who did the breaking up. I think she would have been fine with it if she had been the first to do it. She acted insulted." He shrugged. "I hadn't expected her to be so angry. It was like she was showing her true colours, and I didn't like what I saw. Not that she wasn't great," he hurriedly added. "But she showed a side of her that was...not so great."

"Everybody has more than one side," I said with a smile, hoping to put him at ease. "Was that what you wanted to tell me? That she had an affair with you?"

"Not just that. She had told me she was pregnant when I broke up with her. I think she said it so I would stay with her and take care of her. I think that's what she wanted. Someone with money and a steady job. Someone who didn't treat her as badly as Johnny did. I think she wanted to be saved. But to me it had just been a fling. And I didn't believe her when she told me she was pregnant."

"I'm guessing she didn't take that well either."

"She admitted not being pregnant but was adamant that I would be crawling back to her." He smiled wryly.

"Is that why you'd been talking with her in the garden at the Pembroke?"

"I didn't kill her!" he said loudly, causing some of the other patrons to look up.

"We're rehearsing for a play," I said just as loud.

David looked at me sheepishly. "Thanks. But I really didn't."

"I don't mean on the night of her murder. I mean, earlier."

"Oh. That. Yeah. She handed me a flower and I handed it back to her. She was trying to charm me. To be honest, it was making me question my decision, but then she started flirting with that redhead and Miles and it made me see her for who she really was. Very manipulative."

"Who do you think strangled her?"

He paled slightly at my question. "I really don't know. Lately, she had been saying something about a big break and that she'd be getting a lot of money."

"And she didn't say why?"

"No. She just smirked when I asked about it, like it was some secret. She liked secrets."

Apparently so.

"Who else did she hang out with apart from all of you at The Dramateers?"

He shrugged. "No clue. But I don't think she had many friends. She only texted her husband, and I never heard her talk about anyone else or see her with anyone else. Even during the shows, there was never anyone in the audience that she knew. Not even her husband visited our performances."

"Wasn't that weird?"

"Yes, of course. Once, when she was looking particularly spaced out, I asked her if she was okay and she said that she sometimes felt like she lived in a cocoon, waiting to become a butterfly, and it was the saddest thing I've ever heard."

I nodded slowly. "Especially since we know she never got the chance to become one."

WHEN I RETURNED TO Castlefield, I didn't feel like going back to the bookshop and instead stopped by the vicarage. On my way I spotted Pandora chasing a woman with a toddler. I swear, during the month of Halloween, she got way more evil.

Eleanor was in the kitchen baking an apple cinnamon pie. Her entire cottage smelt like it. A ginger cat purred gently on the rocking chair by the crackling fireplace and we sat down in the living room. The pie was in the oven, but she had grabbed us both a scone with clotted cream and jam and I'd put down the teapot for us.

"I knitted Marjorie a scarf and handed it to her today," Eleanor said.

Marjorie lived in one of the cottages close to the vicarage. Her husband had left her two months ago.

"Did she appreciate it?" I asked.

"She cried. Poor thing."

Before we could gossip any further, Harold wheeled himself into the room and brightened at the sight of me. His grey hair was damp from the rain and he had a plastic bag from the local convenience store on his lap. "Maggie," he said with a beaming smile. "Let me put this away and I'll join you ladies."

"And get yourself a scone," Eleanor called after him.

"As if I need prompting," he called back from the kitchen.

"How are things going with you? When is your new book out?"

"It will be a while, I'm afraid. I've sent a draft to my editor again. Fingers crossed." I took a sip of Earl Grey.

"And the ghastly murder? Have they found the culprit yet?"

"Working on it."

"What's this about the murder?" Harold wheeled in and positioned himself across from the sofa and close to the warm fire. "How are you doing? It must have been awful finding a body. Again."

I winced. "Yeah. I do seem to have a knack for it, don't I?"

He shrugged. "It's not like you're doing it on purpose, but I am quite worried about what people are capable of. I can't imagine anyone thinking that murder is a way out."

"Neither can I," I said. "But not everyone is like us."

"True. It takes all sorts. I suppose sins are part of humanity, but I have trouble accepting them all."

He had never said anything like this before. "I think that's a good thing, Harold."

His smile was weak. "And with the robberies as well. It's very disconcerting."

I perked up. "Robberies? Plural?"

"I figured our own Nancy Drew was the first to know," Harold said, surprised.

"Yes, I thought you knew too. Otherwise I would have said," Eleanor added.

I shook my head. "What happened? Who got robbed this time?"

"This time it was someone's home. I didn't recognise the name. It was a middle-aged woman who lives on the other side of the village and apparently is from a wealthy family. They took all of her jewellery and her iPad and laptop. It happened an hour ago, in broad daylight."

"Who? Did she get a description?"

"She said they were three men, not too big. They had guns," Harold said this time.

My eyes widened. "Guns, really?"

Eleanor shook her head. "Very worrisome, indeed. This is supposed to be a village where you can leave your backdoor un-locked."

"I've stopped doing that since the first murder," I said.

"Good. You might be at more risk since you're known as our local sleuth." Harold winked at me.

"Yes. Goody for me."

Chapter Twenty-One

When I returned to the bookshop, the lovely ladies of the local book club were all there, except my aunt, Olivia and Eleanor.

"I assume you are on the case of the robberies," Lily said as a greeting. She narrowed her eyes at me as if to dare me to defy her.

"I just found out," I said, not really answering her.

"We want to help," Ava said.

"Yes. Before we're next," Jessica added. She clutched her handbag tightly to her chest, as if she was worried it was going to be snatched out from under her any second.

"I admit I'm worried about it too. These people need to be caught soon," I said.

"So we can throw them in prison where their bones will rot until eternity," Poppy said ominously, a dark expression in her watery eyes. "Do you have any biscuits?" she added in a cheerful tone.

We all blinked at her.

"Over there," I pointed to the snug armchairs by the warm drinks machine. There was always a plate with biscuits.

In Poppy's place was a cloud of dust as she dashed over with the speed of a Tasmanian devil.

"So," Lily said. "What's the plan?"

They all looked at me with anticipation.

"Right," I said, struggling to come up with anything. My mind was still on the murder and this new information about the robberies was still being processed.

"Quick," Detective Black said. "Talk about the mating habits of sea urchins."

I cleared my throat.

"Ladies," Alistair's voice sounded behind me.

I turned around to greet him, but the group of women pushed past me and immediately assaulted him with questions about the robbery. They ranged from queries about what was being done to ensure they were safe, to what kind of weapons could be brought during patrol. The latter was being asked by Ava, who took out a list of weapons she hypothetically wanted to bring with her.

Alistair raised an eyebrow at me and I couldn't help but smile at the silliness.

"Ladies," he said calmly and with an authoritative tone. "The cases are being investigated. I'd urge you to stay out of harm's way." He eyed me as he said that.

It would be pointless, though. Those women craved excitement like Pandora craved the screams of her victims.

Which meant that it was probably best if I came up with a harmless plan that should keep them busy. Ava's idea to patrol wasn't actually bad. Then again, what would happen if they did actually witness a robbery taking place? Not that I expected anything like that to happen twice in the same day.

"How about this?" I said loud enough to get their attention. "I think it's important we work closely with the police on this, as not to get our wires crossed." I shot a warning glance at Alistair. He had to play along. "I will go over to Alistair's tonight and come up with a foolproof plan that we can execute tomorrow morning. We will meet back here at my shop at nine. Today, you all get to take the day off. It's going to be hard work." I opted for a grave expression.

"Yes, sir," Ava said and saluted me.

Even Lily seemed pleased with this.

They all started chatting excitedly and left the bookshop talking about what spy equipment they were going to order off the internet.

I let out a sigh.

"Annoying when someone wants to investigate something dangerous even though it's not their business, isn't it?" he said with a smirk.

"Don't be cheeky, now. Or I'll be forced to keep all the clues I gather to myself."

"Does that mean you have uncovered anything?"

"How about we talk about it tonight?" I asked. "Dinner at your place?"

"Hmm. I don't feel like cooking. Is it okay if we order sushi?"

"It is. I'll bring dessert. It may be pure business, but we need dessert."

"Pure business, huh? I'm not sure I can manage that. What would I do with all my carefully prepared banter?" There was a twinkle in his eyes.

"I see. That would be a shame, yes. I suppose a little bit of banter would be okay."

"What a relief," he said dryly.

I chuckled.

Alistair left and I went through the door marked Private when the doorbell to my flat rang. I opened the door to find Stanley there. My cheeks flushed as I recalled the last time I saw him.

"A bit too much of him," Detective Black murmured in my ear.

"Maggie," he said, and cleared his throat three times. He also stared at my shoulder and earlobe instead of looking into my eyes.

"May we speak?"

I stepped back to let him in and sat down on one of the steps, but since he remained standing, my eyes were level with his waist. I quickly got to my feet and aimed for a casual lean against the banister. My elbow slipped past it and I stumbled.

"So, err, is everything okay?" I asked.

His round face started to adapt a similar colour to his cherry sauce. "I realise that you saw me at the art class," he said and cleared his throat a few more times. "The people who follow that class are actually from another village. I don't think I could have done it if it were people who see me every day. But I wanted to do it to be more comfortable in my own skin and I like it. I didn't tell Olivia because it's kind of a private thing, and I didn't want it coming out. People would just make fun and it's too precious to me. Does that make sense?"

I hadn't expected such an explanation. Actually, I hadn't expected any explanation. I also, much to my shame, recalled the reaction me and Alistair had had to seeing him like that. He was right: people would make fun of him. "I totally understand. I'm sorry we burst into the church. We were looking for a...raccoon." I panicked.

Great.

"Ha. And you call yourself a writer," Detective Black said. "Great imagination."

"It's because Olivia asked you to follow me, isn't it?" he asked.

I made a high-pitched noise in the back of my throat as I tried to think of the best reply. Would it be worse or better if I admitted I just wanted a nice distraction from the murder?

"Don't worry about it. I was just hoping you would tell her that I'm not having an affair."

"I already did. I rang her this morning."

His eyes widened. "What did you tell her about what I was doing?"

"Nothing. I told her you weren't cheating and anything else she wanted to know, she would just have to ask you. And you should just tell her. She'll understand. In fact, I think she'll be very happy for you."

He made a face. "I doubt it. She's already embarrassed if either of us wear swimsuits."

"Just because they're married," Detective Black said, "doesn't mean they have to share everything."

I sighed. "I understand. Then why don't you tell her you're part of an art class? You don't have to specify that you're the model."

He perked up at that and even smiled. "Yes, that would be perfect. Thank you, Maggie. And please, don't tell anyone else about this."

"Your secret is safe with me. I promise."

He gave me a shy smile. "Well, I guess this means I owe you a free slice of cheesecake next time you come in."

"No, you don't need t—cheesecake? Okay." I grinned at him.

Stanley chuckled and patted me on the shoulder. "See you around."

"Take care. I'll stop by soon for that cheesecake and some of your buns."

He froze at the door and I realised what I'd said.

Detective Black couldn't hold in his laughter.

Instead of turning around, Stanley simply opened the door and left.

I let go of the breath I was holding. "Note to self, do not mention Stanley's buns. Ever."

Detective Black was still laughing.

Chapter Twenty-Two

It was exactly six o'clock when I rang Alistair's doorbell. He had three pumpkins—uncarved, how dare he?—at the side of his door. His front garden was neatly kept and only contained a few small bushes and plants. I had seen his back garden and that's where he really let loose. Now that it was autumn, though, the colourful flowers were in hiding.

He appeared to really enjoy village life: the gardening, the knitting, the checking on his elderly neighbours. Eleanor had told me he visited both Beth and Poppy regularly and even bought them groceries sometimes. It seemed to me a good thing that he was single so he could explore these things about himself.

Alistair opened the door in a dark orange pullover and grey black trousers.

"Are you supposed to be a pumpkin?" I asked.

"I figured I'd get in the spirit of things." He flashed me a crooked smile.

"I'm so proud of you," I said sarcastically.

"That means so much to me," he returned.

He led the way to the kitchen where he had poured us a sweet white wine, or so he said. He knew I didn't like wine so this was his way of easing me into it.

"I've already ordered, I hope that's okay. I just wanted them to be here quickly in case you were hungry."

My mouth started watering. "I am, good call." I pulled out a chocolate mousse that I had bought on my way over. I held it up. "I saw it and thought, I mousse have that!"

His whole face lit up as he laughed. "I'll have to remember that one."

"Why? Are you planning to shout it at a dinner party? I don't see you doing that."

"Hey, you'll be surprised what I'd do." He got a little closer. "Oh yeah?"

"Yeah. The other day there was music on in that clothing shop behind the post office, and I actually bobbed my head."

I gasped dramatically. "I can't believe it. You really do like to live dangerously."

We grinned at each other.

The doorbell went. "Okay, sit down," he said. "I'll be your server and your chef tonight."

"Okay." I sat down at the kitchen table. There was one red candle in the middle.

"Ooh la la," Detective Black said.

Alistair disappeared into the hallway and later returned with a white bag. He got all the boxes out and put them on the table. He had thought of everything and had gotten all kinds of sushi.

"So, what did you want to discuss?" he asked. "Or do you want to dig in first?"

"No, it's okay. First of all, I think I was wrong about Elijah being trouble. I think it's just my suspicious mind getting the best of me."

"Why do you say that?"

I told him about the necklace and that it turned out to be nothing.

"I looked into Elijah and didn't find out anything troublesome. He was expelled once for getting into a fight. Apparently he was helping his other friends. The crowd he hangs out with seems to be a bit more trouble, though. They've been expelled multiple times and have been caught for vandalism in the past."

I thought about the expensive necklace that a normal teenager wouldn't be able to afford. "Do you think those friends could be involved in those robberies?"

"That's a big leap, Maggie. I'm not investigating the robberies, but I can maybe find out if those boys are persons of interest. Even if they are, it might not make much of a difference. You can warn someone all you want, but some girls like dangerous guys. Or the other way around."

I chewed on my bottom lip. "True. That thought had crossed my mind."

He placed his hand on my wrist. "Try not to worry. We don't know enough to worry yet. And if it turns out that Elijah is bad news, we'll both talk to Emblyn."

I smiled at Alistair. "That's so sweet. Thank you."

He nodded at me.

"This sushi is really good," I said. "Did you find out anything about Warren and Johnny?"

Alistair straightened. This meant he had indeed found something important. "Quite. It turns out that Warren got into a fight with Johnny when he saw him hit Valerie."

"He hit her?"

Alistair nodded. "There were some old bruises on her body. I already figured Johnny had caused those. I just didn't have any proof. Warren witnessing him hitting her allowed me to bring Johnny in for questioning and grill him. Unfortunately, I didn't get anywhere with him. I need evidence if I want to pin him for the murder."

"Why didn't you tell me Johnny beat her? I mean, I know you don't have to, but—"

"Because he would have become your number-one suspect as well, and I didn't want you anywhere near him. I still don't. The only reason I'm telling you now is so that you know we've got this investigation covered. Johnny is on our radar and we'll get him. It's only a matter of time."

"But if he killed her, why did he show up at The Dramateers like that?"

"He's a violent man. It's possible he regretted killing her in a fit of anger and this is how he copes. By blaming others."

I sighed. "Well, did David tell you about the affair when you talked to him?"

Alistair narrowed his eyes at me. "No. When I talked to him, he simply told me Valerie had spoken about getting some money, but nothing else. His bank records also don't show anything suspicious. But you're saying he was having an affair with Valerie? And he told you this?"

"Yes. And he did." I summarised everything he had told me.

"When you say he told you, does that mean you were on your own?"

"We met in a public place. It was fine." I took a bite of a sushi roll with salmon, hoping my casual attitude would transfer to him.

He put down his drink and glared at me.

Alas, one can hope.

"I was with a lot of other people who were also in the pub." I flashed him an innocent smile.

"I know you were careful, but I still don't like it."

I nodded. And I knew why. But just because his former partner died, didn't mean I would.

Alistair stared at his chopsticks. "I know bad things happen and that those things are out of our control, but the fact that they are scares me. It means that at any moment you could cross the street and get hit by a car. I just don't like that."

"I know. But you can't live your life surrounded by bubble wrap or worry all the time. Life is to be enjoyed, remember?"

"Yes, but when you see death as much as I do, it just makes me lose hope sometimes."

"Give it long enough. This village will cure you. It's filled with lovely people and good friends. If you focus on the negative, then it makes sense that's all you see. Try focussing on all the good things. There's a lot of beauty, not just in this village itself, but in the people." I chuckled. "I sound like a Hallmark card."

"No, it's what my therapist said as well, that I should focus more on the good things in life and pick up a few hobbies."

"And have you?"

"Yes. I enjoy knitting now, as well as cooking and gardening, though the latter is more fun in summer."

"What about something physical? Like hiking? We could do that together, maybe. I want to become fitter and stronger."

"That's a good idea. We do have lovely woods here." His eyes glistened. "Also, I still have to teach you how to knit. Why don't we do that after dinner?"

"Okay."

Detective Black scoffed. "First you lie about knitting and who knows what the next lie will be? You might end up saying you don't like cheesecake."

That would be blasphemy.

Alistair told me that Brenda had printed a new flyer because the show must go on and they had made back-up pictures because Brenda was the understudy. Alistair had also gotten Geoff to tell him that the Golden Goose hotel visits were because he was trying to woo a new client. Alistair had confirmed that this was the truth.

It was still obvious how Brenda had cared very little about Valerie, though Geoff I wasn't so sure about. Perhaps none of the members had cared much for her, not even David.

Dinner was lovely and afterwards we took a cup of tea into the study and sat down in the armchairs by the bookcases as Alistair showed me his knitting basket. Him even having one made him ten times more adorable. I didn't know why, but it just did. He helped me pick out the colour of the wool for my scarf—it was the easiest to knit. I made a face.

"I don't really want to knit a scarf," I said.

He gave me a look. "If I stopped using items that were used as murder weapons, I'd never use a knife or a wardrobe."

"A wardrobe?" I frowned.

"It's a long story. Anyway, you're knitting a scarf and that's final."

"Yes, sir."

He sat next to me and gently showed me how to cast on and knit stitch. He was very patient and occasionally had his hands over mine. It wasn't until an hour later that I went on my way. I wanted to stay longer, but that was probably why it was a good idea to leave.

We hugged goodbye and Alistair stood in the doorway until I was completely out of sight. I enjoyed spending time with Alistair and was happy we were friends. Yet my heart still beat a little faster every time we hugged. It had been a few months now since we'd decided to just be friends. Maybe we were both ready. How would I know?

I made my way over to the bridge close to my flat and bookshop. I was looking forward to taking a shower and reading in bed.

Just then a car's tyres screeched as it sped up. It happened so fast that it missed me by a hair's breadth when I jumped out of the way and hit the pavement. The car sped on without its lights on.

Chapter Twenty-Three

The car was out of sight by the time I got to my feet. My hands were scraped and stung, but I was otherwise fine.

"That's not a good sign," Detective Black said. "Or maybe it is. It means you're getting close to the truth."

I was about to reply that I had serious doubts that was the case, nor that we could know if this was related to the murder, when Harold shouted my name. He moved swiftly in his wheelchair as he navigated the cobbled street to get to me.

"Are you okay?" he asked, his face paler than usual.

"Yeah, I think so. Did you get a look at the car?"

"I heard the tyres and wheeled over. It was too dark to make out anything by the time I reached the road. Are you sure you're okay? It sounded as if the car was actually speeding up."

"Err, yeah. I really am fine. I heard it accelerating and just dove out of the way." I looked down the street. It was quiet and I had serious doubts that anyone else but Harold had seen anything useful. Was this really related to the murder? It had to be, but I didn't get it. What kind of threat did I pose? I hadn't really figured anything out and had only talked to three people so far.

"Little bit of a coincidence that this happened after speaking to David," Detective Black said.

"Come, dear. I'll get you some tea at the vicarage. Eleanor has the book club over."

"No, no. They'll just make a fuss. Really I'm fine."

Harold gave me a stern look. "I think a fuss is exactly what you need. You could have died. You do realise that, don't you?"

I bit my lip. "I'm sure it was just an accident."

"Speeding up is hardly that." He squeezed my hand and then led the way to the vicarage. We weren't far from it. My mind was racing. It had happened so fast, I mean, the car was gone just like that. I checked the broken skin on my hands. If it was someone related to Valerie's murder, how had they known where I was? Had they been following me all day perhaps? Or was this just chance?

"It could have been that they were on their way to see you and spotted you walking," Detective Black said. "But the car came from behind. It was pretty impressive of them to recognise you. Unless they had been following you or lying in wait."

Hmm. Food for thought. My least favourite kind of food.

We used the back entrance and entered the kitchen. We were greeted with laughter, which instantly made me feel better. Then again, Harold and Eleanor had always been there for me, so I associated their home with happiness and love.

There were more voices coming from the living room, but Eleanor, Olivia and Poppy were in the kitchen. They were preparing a tray with drinks—mostly wine, and slices of cake on another tray. Poppy was already eating one. There were crumbs on her purple blouse.

"Oh, Maggie, what a lovely surprise. Joining our book club meeting? We're reading a vampire book." Olivia picked up a glass of red wine. "Sat is vy ve're drinking blood," she said in a very fake accent.

I smiled and then realised my legs were shaking.

"Maggie was nearly hit by a car," Harold said in his grave sermon voice. He managed to sound calm, but the fact that he was still pale and his lips were pulled slightly down betrayed his anger.

"I'm really okay," I said, feeling less like I was. I thought back to Alistair and his fear of me dying. He'd even mentioned me getting hit by a car minutes before I was nearly run over.

All the women gasped, causing Poppy to cough up the crumbs she'd inhaled.

Olivia patted her gently on her back.

"Are you okay?" Eleanor asked.

"I'm good," Poppy said with a final cough.

"No, I mean Maggie." She pulled me into a hug and checked me over. "Your hands are scraped."

"I know. But I'm okay, just a bit shaky."

"What happened?"

"The car was speeding up and swerved towards her," Harold said, this time his voice rising with each word.

The voices from the adjacent room quieted and a moment later my aunt Nancy walked in, followed by Ava, Lily, Phoebe, and Jessica.

"What's going on?" Ava asked in her Scottish accent. "Ooh, is there another murder? Do you need our help with it?"

"No," Eleanor said sternly. "Maggie was nearly killed by a car."

I glanced at Nancy who pressed her red lips together and curled her hands into fists. "You were what?!"

"It's okay," I started to say but their reactions hadn't helped me calm down and reality began to sink in, so instead of fake reassurances my bottom lip started to tremble and I began to cry.

Eleanor pulled me into a hug again and stroked my back while a moment later I felt more arms around me. This was exactly why I loved this village so much: my family was here.

WE WERE SEATED IN THE living room a while later. I was sipping on some lemon tea. Strangely enough, I wasn't in the mood for cake, but I figured that would soon change. Not having an appetite was just not my thing.

The women—in the meantime—had gone a little overboard. Eleanor had pulled out a map of Castlefield which showed all the roads in the village but also all the roads leading out of it. Eleanor, Olivia, Lily and Ava were now all marking—but mostly yelling—where all the shops with cameras were. Spoiler: there were only a few. Somehow this had managed to last ten minutes. It had allowed Poppy to covertly eat four slices of cake—and even stuffing two in her handbag, while Jessica and Phoebe were interrogating Harold on what he'd seen. Which hadn't been much.

Nancy was pacing up and down with stomping feet while muttering curses under her breath.

They eventually turned their attention to me as they wanted me to recap everything that had happened in relation to the murder case. Ava had grabbed pens and paper in order to make a suspect list. Apparently Eleanor and Harold's living room was turning into investigation headquarters.

I told them about our visit to Brenda and Geoff and my more recent visit to David and what clues that had generated.

I didn't tell them about Valerie's husband because Alistair had told me to keep it on the down-low, but Ava already put him on the suspect list since Valerie had been cheating. And because he was a man—Ava's words, not mine.

It wasn't that she didn't like men, she just didn't trust them.

"Brenda and Geoff came to the Pembroke by public transport because of the roadworks. Though technically whoever tried to run me over could have taken the long way into Castlefield." I sighed. "It's going to be impossible to find out. Besides, we're not even sure this has anything to do with the murder case. It could have been...something else."

It didn't sound convincing even to me.

They turned back to the coffee table which was hidden by the map, notebooks, and a plate with nothing but crumbs.

"Perhaps there are some traffic cameras on this road," Olivia said and marked an area.

"We'll ask Alistair to check it out," Lily said. "The same with these shops, including Maggie's own. They all have security cameras that also show part of the road. If he was going to visit her, maybe he passed it."

"No!" I suddenly shouted.

They turned their heads in my direction.

"You can't tell Alistair. Just please, trust me. He's already so worried about me. We can solve this without him."

"Maggie, you can't—" Harold started, but Eleanor interrupted.

"We'll take it into consideration. That's all we promise," she said as she gave me a look. I wasn't sure what kind of look it was, but all I could do was nod.

Nancy had started stomping even louder. "This is unacceptable." She turned around and headed for the front door.

"Where are you going?" I asked.

"To find whoever did this and feed them to Pandora." She left without looking back.

I shot a panicked look at Eleanor.

"I'll go," she said, and rose to her feet.

"Me too," said Ava. "Lily, you make a list of potential witnesses we can question. And Poppy—"

Poppy was snoring in her seat.

She sighed. "That woman," she muttered.

I let out a giggle which sounded more nervous than relaxed.

Ava and Eleanor left to make sure Nancy wouldn't murder anyone while Harold went into the kitchen to make a fresh pot of tea.

"We really should do something about the crime rate in this village," said Phoebe.

"Yes, we should protest or make a petition," Jessica added.

"A petition for less...murder?" I asked.

"Exactly," they said simultaneously.

Lily edged closer to me while the two neighbours came up with plans to reduce crime in Castlefield.

"Who do you think did this, Maggie? Surely even you must have some idea," she said.

I narrowed my eyes at her. "Geoff and Brenda seemed to know my reputation as a sleuth, and I'm pretty sure they told the other members of their drama club. That also means that if one of them was worried, they could have decided they wanted to try to kill me. Or it could be that they wanted to talk to me, then saw me walking and took a more violent approach. I don't know. It could be that whoever did it was worried about something they had said to me, but then it would have to be Geoff, Brenda or David. That is still three people to choose from."

"Let's start with them and rule them out until one remains."

I raised an eyebrow. "That's impressive. That's what a detective would do," I said.

She blushed. "Yes, well, you're not the only one who can think like one."

"I'm glad. I can use all the help I can get."

Her expression softened and she placed her warm hand on my knee. "Don't worry. We won't let anything happen to you."

I smiled at her. "Thank you."

IT WASN'T UNTIL AN hour later that Nancy returned. I figured Nancy had convinced Ava and Eleanor to have a look around, and they seemed to be more relaxed when they returned. They didn't say anything, though, so I figured they hadn't discovered anything useful. I wasn't surprised.

Lily had proven to be quite useful and we had brainstormed ideas on how to figure out which of the three drama club members had anything to do with the attempt on my life, and so far we had only come up with ways to check out what kind of car they had. Simply visit them tomorrow morning during their rehearsal. Lily was still convinced that someone must have seen something, and would ask certain nosy neighbours if they'd seen any suspicious vehicles speeding through the cobbled streets.

Any other plans we'd come up with involved bluffing or goading The Dramateers to get them to confess. I definitely wanted to save that as a last resort because it was highly likely that I might need more information from them in the near future. Making them my enemies would not help grease their vocal cords.

The book club meeting hadn't exactly turned out how any of them thought, but they seemed quite energised by it all. I wished I could have said the same, but instead I was yawning my head off.

"Come on," Nancy said as she helped me out of the armchair. "We're having a sleepover. Text Christina so she knows."

"Okay," I said. "That actually sounds really good." When I was younger and there was a thunderstorm, we would always have a sleepover in her bed. We'd have one candle burning and Nancy would read me a story while we munched on popcorn. It actually made it so that I was hoping for thunder instead of fearing it. I still didn't like it much, but at least I had pleasant associations.

I hugged everyone goodbye and we left. Nancy was surprisingly calm as we walked back to her flat, whereas I kept looking over my shoulder, as if expecting the car to return any moment. That didn't happen and instead I snuggled into one of my aunt's oversized shirts and crawled into bed with her while she lit a candle and read me a bedtime story.

I slept like a log that night.

Chapter Twenty-Four

That Thursday morning Eddie and Christina were at work at the Wicked Bookworm downstairs while I returned to my flat after Nancy had made me a delectable breakfast with pancakes and fruit. I had slept in, so the events from yesterday had affected me more than I had liked to think. It meant I couldn't meet the book club women downstairs and make plans with them, but they would understand. At least I felt a lot better now that Nancy and I had had a good old-fashioned bonding session. I guess we were never too old for any of that.

I also knew I had to inform Alistair and went over that conversation in my head while I was making tea in the kitchen. The doorbell rang twice and once more when I was halfway down the stairs.

"What's wrong?" I asked when I opened the door, expecting some sort of emergency. Perhaps another murder?

Alistair's jaw was tensed. "May I come up?"

"Of course." I had the feeling he either found out about my little brush with death last night or someone else had been murdered.

Upstairs I made him a cup of tea as well and we sat down in the kitchen.

He took out his notebook and flipped it open.

I frowned.

Detective Black popped up next to me. "He only does that when he's questioning someone. You haven't murdered anyone while I wasn't looking, have you?"

I glared at him and turned my attention back to Alistair.

He clicked his pen and gazed at me.

"Did you see the car that nearly ran you over yesterday?" he asked in a level voice. He could have just as easily asked me if I had milk.

I swallowed. Someone clearly had told him. Maybe Nancy and Eleanor when they left us last night. I knew someone had to tell him, preferably me, but yesterday—after that conversation about how he was worried something would happen to me—I just couldn't do that to him. And now he'd found out from someone else.

"No. It happened too fast and it was gone before I could register any more facts other than that it was a car." I cleared my throat. His jaw was still tense, and him not showing any emotions was also an indicator that he was certainly upset.

"And can you describe in your own words what happened?" He said it so formally I almost expected him to add 'Miss Matthews' to the sentence.

"I was walking home and heard a car speed up and instinctively dove out of the way. I fell on the pavement and by the time I was up, the car was already too far away. Harold showed up because he had seen it happen and he took me to the vicarage."

He scribbled something in his notebook. I think it was just for show. Was he trying to prove a point?

"Okay, thank you." He flipped his notebook again and put it in his breast pocket before taking a sip of the ginger tea I had poured us.

"Are you going to talk to Harold next?"

"I already have," he said curtly.

Aha. So that meant he had probably spoken to every member of the book club as well. Why had he saved me for last? Wait, I had only just come home. Did that mean he had spent the entire night interviewing the others? I studied his face. He did have dark circles under his eyes, though they weren't so dark as to be immediately noticeable. I had to look closely.

I felt even worse now. I also felt the desperate need to explain to him that I would have told him. Though ideally when I was eighty and we could both laugh about it.

But he got to his feet without warning, thanked me for my time and left the kitchen. I was frozen in my seat in surprise for a moment, then got up and rushed after him. He was already at the top of the stairs. He abruptly stopped there, causing me to bump into him.

Then he turned around, frowned at me and placed his hands on my face. His thumb stroked my cheekbone as his soft lips pressed against mine.

I automatically closed my eyes and didn't open them when he pulled away, or was on the stairs. Only when the door slammed shut did I come back to reality. My eyelids fluttered open and Detective Black was grinning at me.

SOON AFTER, MOST OF the book club women showed up. I had scribbled out a patrolling schedule and handed it to Ava. It would keep the women occupied and make them feel like they were contributing without putting them at risk. Though if any of them encountered the robbers, the robbers would be the ones at risk.

The women also left me plenty of baked goods, so that was my weight loss plan over.

Detective Black scoffed. "It was hardly a plan."

I spent the rest of the day on the sofa with Snowball hopping around. I alternated between daydreaming and knitting my scarf while the TV was on in the background. I wasn't sure what to think or feel, so I simply enjoyed the flutter of butterflies that had been present ever since Alistair had kissed me—while being sober and awake.

I had lunch alone in the flat and then did some cleaning. I was interrupted twice by Christina and Eddie taking turns to come up and question me about my brush with death. Undoubtedly they had heard about it from Nancy, for which I was grateful, since I didn't want to repeat it. They gave me hugs and I assured them I was fine.

Around dinner time I got dressed in dark jeans and a bright red jumper and headed downstairs. I figured I'd ask Miles to have dinner in the pub again and then planned on following around The Dramateers. I was going to stake-out every single member, which would take days, but I had to do it. If someone really was trying to kill me, I had to solve this before they tried again.

As I opened the door, Miles stood there with his fist raised as if he was about to knock. He grinned and ran a hand through his hair. As he opened his mouth to say something, Pandora's battle cry rang through the air.

Miles's eyes widened and he jumped inside, shutting the door behind him. "That sounded way too close," he said.

I chuckled. "She really did a number on you, didn't she?"

"The only birds I want chasing me are women."

"Even if they're as violent as Pandora?"

"No. If a woman starts pecking at my ankles, it's all over." He said this in such a serious tone that I couldn't help but laugh.

"Really? I thought men appreciated a good lethal attack every now and then."

"Yes. Most men love that but not me. I guess I'm weird." He cracked a smile.

"So, reporting for bodyguard duty?"

He put his hands in his pockets. Somehow he made that look elegant. "Are you alright?"

I shrugged. "I'm alive, so I guess I am. I think Alistair's upset with me."

Miles patted my arm. "He's not, he's just terribly worried. I also think he was hoping you'd confide in him."

"I know. It's not because I don't care about him. In fact, it's because I do that I didn't want to tell him."

Miles sighed. "Of course you meant well, and it's not like you were thinking straight, but if the roles had been reversed, wouldn't you have wanted to do anything you could to help?"

I nodded.

"Don't worry. I'm pretty sure he's already forgiven you."

"Really?"

"Yes. It's you, after all." He smiled.

I felt very sure at that moment that I loved Alistair.

"Finally," Detective Black muttered in the background.

And I had to tell him soon. Fear was stupid and I was done letting it make decisions for me.

"Anyway, I'm hungry. Let's have dinner at the pub and then I'll tell you about my new plan."

"Lead the way, boss," Miles said with a grin.

MILES AND I STARTED off with drinks and chatted until Eddie and Christina showed up. I had texted them and invited them to join us. I was also hoping to bring Eddie along for the first stake-out session as well.

Callum showed up to take our food orders and also to show off part of a dance routine since he was asked to be in a music video that one of his friends was producing. It was for YouTube and not to be broadcast on TV, but apparently his friend had a lot of followers on his channel and it could be big for Callum.

I had to admit, Callum had moves I could only dream of. Granted, I could literally trip over my own feet, but he had wonderful coordination skills. It was as if he was actually in control of his own body. I wondered what that was like.

After Callum had suitably impressed us, he left us to it. We didn't have to wait long for our food. Eddie was the first to finish his plate and provided entertainment by telling us about what had happened at The Wicked Bookworm today.

Phoebe and Jessica showed up and wanted to buy the same book, but there was only one copy and they ended up fighting. They weren't very good at it and just slapped each other's hands, but Eddie still had to break them up. Instead of selling them that book, he sold them each a different book of which there were plenty of copies and they left without bickering. Well, minor bickering.

Lily had also showed up in the late afternoon to buy a book on how to charm people. Something she really needed. And Ava had stopped by for gossip. Luckily she hadn't mentioned the car thing, but she did mention Pandora attacking a couple of nuns that were passing through the village.

See. Demonic.

"There was also a woman who stopped by and asked about you," Eddie said. "She seemed a bit...shady."

Miles and I perked up. "What do you mean, shady?" I asked.

"I don't know. Something was a bit off about her. She asked after you, but I just couldn't imagine you knowing her. I guess that's a bit mean, but I just got a feeling."

"Can you describe her?" Miles asked before I could.

"Short blond hair. Dark eyes. Pale skin. She didn't look too good. I told her you weren't here but didn't feel comfortable telling her you lived above the bookshop and said she should try again tomorrow."

"Good call. I think." I couldn't imagine who it could be and what she would want.

"Do you think it's related to you nearly being run over?" Christina asked.

"I don't see how, but I don't even understand why anyone would want to run me over, so..."

"Maybe you should stop investigating," Christina said.

"We don't even know if it's related to that," I replied. But nearly being run over had taken the wind out of my sails somewhat.

"Are you kidding?" Eddie said, to my surprise. "If it is then I want to stop this bastard. We can't let anyone get away with treating our Maggie like this. I say we put the pressure on all of The Dramateers members."

"I was thinking of staking them all out," I said softly, slightly intimidated by Eddie's passionate response.

"Yes." He slammed the table with his fist. "That is exactly what we should do. We are going to show them that nobody messes with The Super Sleuthers." He had become even more animated.

Callum showed up at our table. "Dessert?"

Eddie flipped a switch and calmly smiled at him. "Yes, please."

I was about to comment on it, when a thought occurred to me. "Hey, Call, do you know anything about the acting club The Dramateers?" I asked him. With his passion for acting, there was a small chance he had heard of them.

He put his hand in his side as he thought about it. "I'm not sure. I'm terrible with names," he said.

I pulled out my phone and went to their Facebook page. I showed a couple of pictures.

"Actually, yeah. But not from acting; I know them from here. They visited the pub about a week ago."

I checked the picture while Callum pointed out Valerie and David.

"What were they talking about?"

"They were fighting. I'm pretty sure he was breaking up with her. I get the feeling it was an affair." He raised his eyebrows at me.

"That would imply that David was telling the truth," I muttered to Miles and Eddie. "Thanks, Callum."

"Happy to help."

We all ordered dessert and switched to a different topic until it was time to go. Christina didn't join us, so it was just us Super Sleuthers, on a new mission.

THE FIRST PERSON I wanted to stake-out for the evening was Brenda. She was currently my number-one suspect.

I borrowed Nancy's Land Rover again and drove us to Brenda and Geoff's home. I figured not much exciting stuff would happen because most people stayed home in the evenings, but it was worth a shot.

We parked opposite their home, Miles in the passenger seat and Eddie in the back.

"Do you have any snacks?" Eddie asked.

"You're hungry already?" Miles turned in his seat.

"Not already. Still. I'm always hungry. It's in my DNA."

"Mine too," I said and handed him my handbag; it was filled with various salty snacks.

Eddie made noises of content while Miles chuckled.

An hour later Eddie was snoring lightly in the back and all the while nothing had changed at Geoff and Brenda's. The light was still on, the curtains drawn. We could vaguely make out shapes every now and then. I wondered what Geoff and Brenda were watching on TV—assuming they were watching TV together.

"What do we expect to happen exactly?" Miles asked. "I mean, what's the point of this?"

"The point is that they won't expect being watched, and I'm hoping to gather more information about all of them."

"I checked out Geoff's website," Miles said. "Then I pretended I wanted to hire him and talked to two of his clients."

My eyes nearly rolled out of my head. "You did? Look at you, sleuthing."

A smug smile appeared on his face. "I am a super sleuther, after all. Anyway, his clients were happy with his work, but it seems he's dropped a few clients in favour of wealthier ones."

"I see. Maybe h—" I started, but out of the corner of my eye I caught movement and spotted Geoff leaving his home. He wore a black hat and a striped scarf.

It wasn't too late, but I still couldn't help but wonder where he was off to at this time.

"Something innocent or nefarious?" I asked.

"Only one way to find out," Detective Black said.

Chapter Twenty-Five

Geoff didn't take his car, so we decided to follow him on foot, much to Eddie's dismay; he was forced to leave any and all snacks behind.

"You know, maybe I should stay in the car. My hair does stand out," he tried as we walked along the sidewalk.

"You wish," I said.

He puffed up his cheeks in indignation. "Hey, it does. When I was seven, Mary-Sue didn't want to go steady because she said that I reminded her of a freckled tomato."

"That's mean," Miles said.

"I know. Joke was on her, though, because that summer holiday she ended up sunburnt and looked bright red for weeks. My classmates called her Lobster the entire year. Not me, of course."

Around that time I was still living with my parents and didn't have many friends because by that time my mother was already known for being...eccentric. The kids in my class acted as if mental illness was contagious. At first I hated the idea of coming to Castlefield and not being with my dad, but I soon loved it. Eddie was a huge part of that.

We continued following Geoff at a respectable distance. Far enough he wouldn't immediately be able to make us out, but close enough not to lose him.

"Do you remember when you tried making balloon animals for me that following year? It was the first year we were classmates and the teacher had invited a balloon person—I don't know what you call it."

"I think he referred to himself as a balloon artist," Eddie said with a smile.

"Right. Well, I was so excited by what he could do that you brought balloons the following week and blew them up, which took you forever, and then tried making animals."

"You did?" Miles glanced at Eddie with a raised eyebrow.

Eddie shrugged. "She'd really liked them."

I chuckled. "You ended up popping three of them and the other shapes you made resembled blobs. Drunken blobs."

Miles laughed at this.

"I did my best."

"True," I said and put my arm around him. "I appreciate that. It's what made us friends."

Eddie smiled. "Yeah, you're right. I forgot that was what sealed the deal."

"Okay, this was pointless." Miles abruptly came to a stop. I bumped into him.

"What is?"

Miles pointed at the pub Geoff entered.

"Great, he's just going for a pint." Eddie sighed.

"We don't know that." I hurriedly crossed the street to make it over to the pub, but stayed to the side of the building. Miles and Eddie followed me.

"What? You think he's meeting someone?" Miles asked from behind me as I peered through one of the windows. There was a couple sitting by the window that didn't even notice.

"Not necessarily, but what if he is? Then I'd like to—Oh, there he is. Look, isn't that David?" I pointed towards the bar, but Miles and Eddie would have to press themselves to the window in order to spot them, like I was.

The couple by the window looked up just as I was about to tell Miles and Eddie to look. They visibly startled and I waved apologetically. Then I backed away and out of sight.

"So, Geoff is meeting his drama buddy David. The one that had been having an affair with Valerie. Do you think they do this all the time or that they have something to discuss?" I wondered out loud.

"I'll find out," Eddie said and made his way to the door.

"Woah." I grabbed his arm. "How?"

"I'll figure something out, don't worry. I do my best work while improvising."

"You do?" I frowned.

"Yeah." He smiled at us and went inside.

"Should we be worried?" Miles asked.

"I think we should be a little worried."

A few seconds later Eddie walked out with a triumphant smile on his face.

"What—how are you here so quickly?" I felt the worry in the pit of my stomach increase tenfold.

"They apparently meet up regularly," he said. "I asked the bartender. He recognised them."

"Smart," Miles said with a nod.

"So David and Geoff are pretty good friends." I filed away that information. I wasn't sure if it was important yet.

"Does this mean we're done? I'm cold." Eddie pouted.

"You just want to go back to where the snacks are." I punched him on the arm.

"And where my game controller is." Eddie looked at Miles who got the message and looked at me.

"Sure, let's go so you guys can game."

We walked back to the car while Miles and Eddie discussed gaming strategies.

THE NEXT MORNING IT was time for my next stake-out session, and this time I'd be on my own.

Detective Black coughed loudly.

And with my loyal detective.

Geoff would be working, but when I had looked into Brenda, I had discovered that she had recently quit her job as a librarian. Recently, as in a few days ago. I thought the timing was odd.

So I was back at their home the next morning. At first, it was very quiet, but I'd brought my notebook for some book plotting.

Brenda left her home around eleven o'clock in the morning to get groceries, then she left about an hour later to visit a beauty salon where she stayed almost two hours, driving me insane with boredom.

She left the beauty salon not particularly looking any different, but if Christina had been with me, she would have undoubtedly noticed. Next, I followed her to expensive-looking boutiques before she finally ordered something to go from a coffee place in Woolfield and took a stroll through a nearby park.

Woolfield was slightly bigger than Castlefield, and in my opinion Castlefield was a lot more cosy than this village. Of course Woolfield had one amazing thing that we did not: the lack of a vindictive winged monster.

I parked the Land Rover and got out. The wind was colder than yesterday and I pulled up my collar. Perhaps it was time to hurry up and buy a new scarf.

Brenda was on top of a bridge overlooking a small pond in the middle of the green grass and wooden benches. Ducks were drawn to the bridge, hoping that Brenda brought some snacks, but all she did was sip her hot beverage and stare at the water.

There was a jogger in the park, as well as a few young families and people passing through.

"Hey," I said as I approached her.

Her made-up eyes widened as she noticed me. "Maggie, right? What a surprise to see you here." She looked different than before. Her make-up heavier, as was her perfume. She had put down the handful of shopping bags and her eyes darted down to them.

"I was in the neighbourhood," I said with a smile.

"Yes," Detective Black said. "It is always better to make them lower their guard."

Not that I believed that Brenda ever did that. Not truly.

"Are you still looking into that poor girl's death?" There was a sharpness in her tone that she failed to hide.

"I am. She was killed with my scarf."

She narrowed her eyes. "What was she doing wearing your scarf?"

"I guess she was cold."

Brenda sniffed. "She liked to take what wasn't hers." Then she looked away, as if she wanted to hide her expression.

It wasn't as if I was surprised. She clearly hadn't liked Valerie and she certainly wouldn't have approved of her having an affair with David.

"I'm sorry you lost your job," I said. "As a librarian."

She frowned at me. "How do you know about that? You know what, it doesn't matter. Why are you bringing it up? What exactly are you accusing me of?"

I smiled again. "I'm sorry. I didn't mean to make you feel like I was accusing you. I was just wondering why you quit your job. As a writer I love libraries, and librarians do important work."

At this, she looked more pleased. Her shoulders drooped and the corners of her mouth turned upwards. "Thank you. I did enjoy it, I suppose. But it's not my dream. Acting is my dream. And I wasn't fired. I quit."

"You're lucky you can afford to live off one salary then. Everything is crazy expensive."

"Well, Geoff has gotten a few wealthy clients lately so we are both very lucky. It also helps our financial situation that we never had any kids." She regarded me with a cool expression as if daring me to express sympathy.

I simply nodded. "I can understand that. Well, I'm glad you can follow your heart. The new play looks really good and you're very talented."

This time she actually smiled at me. "Thank you. I appreciate that."

"What do you like most about acting?" I asked.

She tilted her head as she considered that, then took a sip of her drink. "That I get to experience what it's like to be someone else."

"That's what I like about writing as well."

She nodded at me. "Artists always understand each other."

Great. Now I was bonding with a murder suspect.

Chapter Twenty-Six

My first stop in Castlefield was my aunt's shop. I went around lunchtime, hoping I could join her. I needed a dose of Nancy.

Emblyn was ringing up a customer who was buying herbal tea and a few candles while Nancy's blonde beehive disappeared behind the half-open door to her flat. Bailey trotted behind her.

I caught the door just before it shut, causing Nancy to look over her shoulder.

"Hey, can I join you for lunch?"

"Does a tea kettle whistle?" She chuckled as we walked up the stairs.

"How are things going with Gus?" I asked when we moved to the kitchen. Her flat was open plan and she had a small cooking island at which I sat down.

"He's doing quite well, actually. Considering. We take walks each evening."

"How romantic," I said.

"It's not romantic when he keeps jumping in puddles, ruining my leggings."

I laughed as I pictured this. "Are you kidding? That's so cute. You should always embrace your inner child."

"I'm plenty in touch with my inner child. And I showed him that when I shoved him into a bush."

I laughed again.

Nancy made us both cups of Tetley's tea and a cheese sandwich and sat down on the bar stool next to me.

"Speaking of romance," Nancy started. "Have you jumped Alistair's bones yet?"

"Nancy! Of course not."

"Well, you should. You never know how long you have." She winked at me to lighten her words.

I took a sip of my tea. She did have a good point there. But first things first.

"We are both preoccupied with this murder," I said.

"Good. Then you can be preoccupied with it together."

I glared at her.

"Naked."

My shoulders shook as I struggled to hold in my laughter. She never had any trouble saying what she thought. The first time I had introduced a boyfriend to her, she had told him he should shave because his attempt at a beard made him look like hadn't washed his face. Luckily, it had made him laugh…and shave. But not everyone could appreciate that type of candour.

It started raining and the sound of raindrops smashing against the window filled the flat. Our tea was warm and our sandwiches filling.

"Emblyn has a date tonight," Nancy said. "With a bloke called Elijah. I haven't met him, but she's so excited that she started talking in a high-pitched voice that only Bailey understood."

Bailey cocked his head and his tail started wagging.

"I'm happy for her. I hope he's good to her."

"Why wouldn't he be?"

"Something I overheard when they were talking. Emblyn mentioned the word trouble. It was something he had invited her for. It just makes me think he's a bit of a bad boy."

"Oh, I love bad boys," Nancy said with a smirk.

I rolled my eyes. "When have you ever dated a bad boy?"

"I'm smart enough to not date them, but I do love them."

I wondered if she had told Gus she loved him. Or if he had told her that. They were clearly in love. What would happen when his health seriously deteriorated? Would they move in together?

"We're carving pumpkins with the book club the night before Halloween. We'll do it at Eleanor's, in case you want to join," Nancy said.

"That sounds like fun. Will there be pumpkin pie?"

She scoffed. "Do you have to ask?"

I grinned.

After we had finished our lunch, we moved to the sofa and finished our tea while I told Nancy about what we'd found out regarding the murder so far.

"Geoff sounds fishy," she said. "Or maybe that's because I don't trust people who are good with numbers."

"Why would you—never mind, go on."

She shrugged. "I'm just saying, it sounds like they both care about wealth and fame."

"You think they care about fame?"

"Of course. He is the leader of that acting group, he's rented the theatre. Just because they're a small, unsuccessful group of actors, doesn't mean they don't want to be big. They probably have big plans and are working hard towards that goal."

"Then why do a silly murder mystery weekend?"

"Miles is easily found on the internet. He's a wealthy attorney and his parents are rich too, aren't they? They probably wanted to get in Miles's good books."

Even so, what would that mean?

"Do you think that Valerie got in the way of that? Or do you think the murder was inconvenient for them? I find it difficult to find out why she's been killed."

Nancy shrugged. "Only the killer knows."

"Unfortunately."

I SPENT THE REST OF the afternoon cleaning the flat and playing with Snowball. I had bought a small ball and rolled it around, making her chase it and hit it with her small nose. She would zoom around the living room and then pounce the ball. It was hilarious.

Around five o'clock I got a text message from Alistair, inviting me to dinner at the pub. I told him I'd be there in twenty minutes and put Snowball in her cage. I changed into a woollen dress and put up my hair. I added a bit of lipstick and left a note for Christina.

I took the back entrance and walked to the pub. It was still raining, but it was a light drizzle and I didn't feel like lugging around a wet umbrella.

The pub wasn't super busy, but it was pretty full already. I enjoyed the sound of comfortable chatter as I walked into the warm establishment. Callum was behind the bar again and gave me a delicate wave that I returned.

Alistair was at a table in the back and smiled when I joined him.

"Had a good day?" I asked as I took off my coat and placed it over the back of my chair before sitting down opposite him.

"I had a busy day, but it ended well enough. I questioned Brenda at the station today. She's our main suspect."

"She is? Why?"

"Because I visited Warren and he told me he had witnessed Brenda slap Valerie after Valerie had told her she was pregnant with Geoff's baby."

I gasped. We already knew that was a lie so she did that just to mess with Brenda. And what a cruel lie, too.

"What did she say when she was questioned?"

"She admitted that it had happened but denied she had killed her."

"She lied to try to get David back, then she lied to hurt Brenda. She was quite something." I shook my head.

"Even so, is it the reason she was killed? Apparently, that incident occurred about a week or so ago. It would be a late response if Brenda really had killed her because of that," Alistair said.

"True."

Then he asked me what kind of drink I wanted and went to the bar to fetch it for me. I took that time to check my small hand mirror and see if my lipstick still looked nice.

I completely understood why Brenda hated Valerie, and I wondered what Geoff's role was in this. Would Brenda have told Geoff about this? Would she have believed it? Was there any truth to it? Geoff had given her all the best roles. Perhaps she had him wound around her finger. Or she'd simply manipulated him, or even blackmailed him. I wouldn't put it past her to have a one-night stand with Geoff and then hold that over him.

Of course, this was all speculation. And getting Geoff to confess to something like that, if it had happened, would be difficult. Valerie was dead, but his wife wasn't. And he wouldn't want her to know.

Alistair returned with a glass of lemonade.

"Do you really think Brenda killed Valerie?" I asked.

He sighed. "The only thing I know is that I don't have any evidence. I had to let Brenda go after questioning her, and it means I'm stuck. You said she mentioned that money was coming in, but there's nothing to find in her bank statements. And even though she's done some awful things, I can't be certain that those were the reasons she was killed."

I nodded. "After dinner I'll go for my next stake-out. Maybe I'll see something that will crack this case."

Alistair's lips tugged into a smile. "As long as you don't go alone, be my guest."

I narrowed my eyes. I knew what he was thinking. He was sure I was just wasting my time, sitting in a car outside someone's home. And I'm sure he was pleased, thinking it kept me out of harm's way.

We chatted for a bit about this and that, and only ordered dinner when Eddie and Miles showed up. Apparently, Alistair had invited them as well.

Detective Black smirked. "Disappointed it's not a date?"

I chose to ignore that.

My thoughts were already at the next stake-out, though. We needed a breakthrough or this killer would get away.

Chapter Twenty-Seven

Johnny lived in a terraced house with a small front garden. The garden was actually well kept and neat. There was a small bush and the rest was tiled. A bench with pumpkins was below the window next to the front door. I couldn't help but wonder if Valerie had put them there.

There was a white van parked in front and I figured it belonged to Johnny. Mainly because his name was on it and it stated he was a plumber. It meant that Johnny was home. It was now nearly seven thirty and I had brought my squad.

"So what's the plan? When do we break in?" Eddie asked from the back seat of Nancy's Land Rover.

Miles and I both turned to him. "Who said anything about breaking in?" I asked.

Eddie raised an eyebrow. "Is this not the plan? How else are we going to gather clues?"

"By observing," I said. "I told you it's a stake-out."

"But how do you know what he's doing? What if he's going to stay inside the whole evening? What if he's doing something nefarious inside? We don't have x-ray vision. I keep putting it on my Christmas list but it never happens."

"I wonder why, it's not like it's an unreasonable request," I muttered.

"Exactly," Eddie said.

I pulled out the bag of snacks and flung it at Eddie. "Get ready for a long evening."

IT WAS NEARING MIDNIGHT and my bum was beginning to get sore.

"You would think you're used to sitting all the time," Detective Black said from the back seat.

I resisted the urge to turn around and stick out my tongue.

"What is your most awkward date?" Eddie asked Miles. In the past hour he had taken turns asking us both questions about our lives. He even asked me questions he knew the answer to, probably to give Miles the insider scoop.

"Why do most of your questions revolve around embarrassment?" I asked him.

"Sh. Just answer the question, Miles." Eddie ate a salt and vinegar crisp.

Miles exchanged an amused glance with me. "It's okay. I've never had embarrassing dates," he replied.

"What?" Eddie leaned forward. "How is that possible? You must have one."

Miles shook his head. "All my dates have been quite successful."

"Define successful," I said, then held up my hand. "No, no. Never mind. I don't want to know."

Miles chuckled.

"Wait," Eddie said. "I want to know." He had a smirk on his face.

"Hang on, look." I pointed to Johnny's front door which had just opened. Johnny locked the door behind him and walked over to his van.

We all lowered ourselves in our seats even if it was too dark for him to see us. There was a street light, but we had parked strategically.

"Where do you think he's heading?" Miles asked.

"Only one way to find out." I started the car and followed him from a safe distance.

"So, Eddie. While we're in a low-speed chase, why don't you tell us what your most embarrassing date is?" Miles said.

"Oh, that's easy." His tone indicated he was actually going to enjoy telling this story. Eddie didn't get embarrassed easily, and when he did, he could laugh about it. I really admired that about him.

"It wasn't a local woman, but she frequented the bookshop a few years ago. She always wore these floral dresses and a cute smile."

I groaned as I realised what story he was going to tell.

Miles chuckled again. "This is going to be good."

"Anyway," he said. "She frequented the shop and always struck up a conversation when she saw me, but I didn't imagine that she liked me because she was super pretty."

"Until she came up to me and asked me if Eddie was single," I said.

"Yep. And then the next time she came in, I tried flirting with her. I say try because I'm not very good at it."

I chuckled. "He always starts talking about global warming when he likes someone. It's very weird."

"I'm just trying to impress her by sounding like I know what's going on in the world, okay?" Eddie said while gesturing with his hands. "Anyway, the next time she came in, she told me to come to come to the pub at a certain time."

I groaned again.

"Is it that bad?" Miles asked me.

I nodded.

"It was," Eddie added. "I show up feeling a bit nervous."

"A bit?" I asked as we drove towards the edge of Woolfield.

"Okay, I nearly threw up because of the nerves I felt. That's because I didn't have much dating experience then."

"And you do now?" Miles asked.

"No. Let's get back to the story. I show up feeling a tad nervous and see her at one of the tables with a teenager. It turns out it's her sister and she's setting me up with her. Apparently I looked seventeen even though at that time I was twenty-four."

I groaned again.

"What are you groaning about? It was awkward for me, not you."

"I can feel the awkwardness seeping through my bones each time you even mention the story."

Miles laughed. "I'll admit it's pretty bad. But let's assume it won't ever be as bad as that again."

"Don't jinx it!" Eddie and I called simultaneously.

We followed Johnny deeper into the woods until he slowed down and parked at the side of the wide dirt path.

"What do I do?" I asked, panicked.

"Keep driving. Stay calm," Miles said. "Just park up ahead and turn off the lights. We'll have to walk back in order to see what he's doing."

"But what if he drives off?" Eddie asked.

"Then we hide until he passes us and follow him in the car again. It's not like there are many roads here. We would catch up to him."

"He sounds as if he's done this many times before," Detective Black said.

"Watch a lot of TV, do you?" I asked him.

He grinned at me.

I did as he instructed and parked far away for Johnny to lose sight of us. We all got out of Nancy's Land Rover and stood in the dark forest. None of us had brought a torch, but it wasn't as if we could use it.

Miles took the lead and we sneaked along the road, making our way back to where Johnny had pulled over. He had his lights still on, forcing us to move off the path and weave our way through the oak trees. Occasionally the chilly autumn air made the dying leaves rustle.

As far as spooky outings went, this one was definitely spooky.

Occasionally a twig snapped under our shoes, but it wasn't anything that Johnny could hear since he was still in his van. We hid behind a large oak tree, close enough to the van that we could hear the thumping of music.

"What do you think he's doing?" I whispered.

"I can't see," Miles muttered. "Maybe he's meeting someone."

"This late? At the side of a road in the middle of the woods?" Definitely suspicious.

"I'm cold. Can we get back to the car and eat snacks? I liked that part," Eddie whispered.

I glared at him, which was unsuccessful because it was too dark for him to pick up on it.

"No," Miles said sternly.

There was silence except for the thumping car radio in Johnny's van.

"I need to pee," Eddie said.

Both Miles and I groaned.

The engine was turned off just as another car came up from behind his. The car drove slowly and stopped right behind Johnny.

"Show time," I whispered and we all crouched. I wasn't sure why; the trees provided enough cover.

"Hey, mate," Johnny said as he stepped out and shut the door behind him.

A man with a ponytail and a black jacket stepped out of his car. I couldn't make out what kind it was. Maybe the guys could.

"What's up?" the other man said. I couldn't detect an accent.

"Same as before?" Johnny asked.

"Yeah." He reached into his pocket and took out a stack of money.

"It's good stuff, eh?" He took the money and counted it.

"Oh, yeah. Makes me fly in the clouds all night."

Johnny chuckled, his voice rough, then opened the back of his van, grabbed a padded envelope and handed it to him. They made the exchange, said goodbye and got in their vehicles. A few seconds later they both drove off. Johnny went straight ahead, the other guy turned around.

Only when the rumble of car engines had completely disappeared did we dare to get up and breathe.

"Wow," I said.

"Was that what I think it was?" Eddie ran a hand through his red hair, making it even messier than usual.

"Yeah. Drugs," Miles said. "Definitely drugs."

IT TOOK THREE RINGS before Alistair answered the door in his kitten pyjamas. He rubbed his eyes. "Where's the fire?"

My mouth dropped. "Those are your pyjamas? They're so cute."

Eddie chuckled while Miles simply looked incredibly serious. He had a line between his perfectly shaped eyebrows and his mouth was pulled into a straight line.

Alistair blushed. "Come in," he said.

As we followed him into the kitchen, I also noticed he wore bunny slippers.

"We went on a stake-out and followed Johnny and it turns out he's dealing drugs," Eddie said as he slid into a chair at the breakfast table. Alistair froze as he made his way to the kettle on the stove.

"You saw this?" He asked as he continued and started preparing tea.

"Yes," we all said at the same time.

I sat down opposite Eddie while Miles took place next to him. Man, I was really tired. I stifled a yawn, prompting Eddie to do the same.

We sat there silently while Alistair brought out a plate of biscuits—yay—and later also the tea.

Eddie munched on the biscuits as if he hadn't been snacking all night.

"What exactly happened?" Alistair asked.

Miles explained what we had seen, sticking purely to facts. He didn't even use the word drugs, though it was implied.

I could see why. He was a criminal defence attorney. Technically we could have seen Johnny exchange pens.

"Valerie had bragged about making a lot of money. It could be that she knew about Johnny doing something illegal—if that's what it was. Perhaps she was even involved," I said.

"I don't suppose you got the license plate from the other car?" Alistair asked.

Eddie and I shook our heads, then Miles rattled off the numbers and letters.

"Wow, impressive," I said.

"I figured it would come in handy," Miles said. He took a sip of his tea, looking quite cool. If you liked that sort of thing. I preferred men in cute pyjamas and bunny slippers.

Chapter Twenty-Eight

After we had finished our tea, Alistair escorted us to the front door.

"I understand you're all eager to solve the mystery, but get some sleep and most importantly, let me get mine," Alistair said with a sparkle of humour in his eyes.

"And deny ourselves the opportunity to see you in your jammies?" I shook my head. "Don't think so."

There was a bright flash and we turned to Eddie who had a triumphant smile on his face.

"I have photographic evidence now," he said.

"And your plan is to do what with that?" Alistair asked.

Eddie tilted his head. "Hm. I'll bet a lot of older women will pay to see this picture."

A shrill whistle cut through the air as we turned our heads to Ava, dressed in a fluorescent vest while holding a baseball bat and wearing face paint—three streaks of green paint as if she was in a warzone. Next to her was Poppy in a similar outfit but instead of a baseball bat, she was holding a jar of liquorice.

"Speaking of the devil," Detective Black muttered in my ear.

They approached the short pathway that led to Alistair's front door.

"What is going on he—" Ava started, but then she realised what Alistair was wearing. "Oh, my. Don't you look adorable."

The light by his front door illuminated his face enough for me to see that he was blushing.

Eddie chuckled to himself.

"What are you guys doing? Shouldn't Poppy be in bed? It's like seven hours past her bedtime," I said.

"I took five naps today so I could join the patrol," she said. "Do you have any sweets on you?"

"No. And what patrol?"

Ava jutted her chin out. "The one you suggested. You said it was a good idea to start patrolling the neighbourhood in order to protect people from those thieves."

Alistair cleared his throat.

I glanced at him. "I didn't exactly say that—it was just an idea..." My voice trailed off. "Wait. Does this mean—" My question was answered when there was another whistle and Lily, Olivia, and Nancy showed up. Nancy was holding her broom, while Lily held a fly swat and Olivia a roller pin.

"Is everything alright? We heard a whistle," Lily asked, slightly out of breath.

"Nice pyjamas," Nancy said with a wink.

Again, Alistair blushed. He stuck out his chin. "They are comfortable," he said.

"Of course they are, dear. I love them," Olivia said.

"Did you uncover any mayhem?" Eddie asked the ladies.

"Well, we discovered that Mr Wimperton pees in his garden when he's drunk," Lily said as she wrinkled her nose. "He will be hearing about that tomorrow. It is just not something that we should allow in this neighbourhood."

"Peeing? No, it's awful," I said.

Lily glared at me.

"What are you all doing here so late? Are you having a sleepover, and if so, why was I not invited? I'm an excellent spooner," Nancy said.

Alistair blushed again. "No, they were just here to say hi. And it looks like you're all keeping the neighbourhood safe. Very impressive. Should I be worried about the 'weapons'?"

"Nah," Nancy said. "They're only a tiny bit lethal."

A whistle cut through the air and the women immediately straightened their backs.

"Someone is in peril!" Poppy shouted, and darted off with the speed of a hunting leopard.

"Bet you regret being in your pyjamas—" Eddie started, but Alistair was as fast as the book club women who ran off in the direction of the blown whistle.

"Let's go," I said, and started as well.

"I'll man the fort," Eddie said and pointed to Alistair's open front door.

"Me too," Miles added with a shrug. Both of them suddenly looked tired.

Not me. Not when there could be a hint of danger. "Okay, I'm sure it's nothing. We'll be right back." I hurried after the group.

We weaved our way through the cobbled streets until we reached the square by the church where the other book club ladies were. I spotted Eleanor, Phoebe, Jessica, and a male teenager, by the looks of it.

At first glance it looked like they were performing a strange ritualistic dance, but as we got closer it became clear that Pandora was making a play for the boy's ankles and the women had formed a circle around him, ensuring he couldn't leave.

"Alistair," Phoebe called out. "Arrest him. He's a thief!"

"Everyone calm down." Alistair's voice was loud and the women stopped moving. Even Pandora froze for a moment, allowing the bloke to make a run for it. He didn't get far.

Nancy swung her broom and hit his leg, causing him to topple forward. He didn't get the chance to scramble to his feet, because Pandora jumped on his back and any attempt at moving was met with a peck on his neck. That kept him frozen in fear while we came closer.

There was a black backpack on the ground. The top was zipped open and a few expensive-looking necklaces had slipped out.

"Pandora was attacking him and we went over to help him but then we saw the jewellery. He's one of the people who's been robbing us," Jessica said. "It's not right. He can't get away with this. Arrest him and throw him in the dungeon."

"We don't have a dungeon in Castlefield, you fool," Ava said.

"Well, we should. I'm going to have a word with the mayor about it. Get a petition started." Jessica folded her arms.

Ava shook her head in dismay. "The mayor gets a stress rash each time you come within ten metres of him."

"Was there anyone else around?" I asked. From what I'd heard, there were three people involved in the home invasion.

"No," Phoebe said.

"Can someone get this monstrous chicken off me?" the boy said through gritted teeth. He had to be about seventeen.

Alistair shooed away Pandora, who obeyed, and he searched him for a weapon before hauling him to his feet.

"What do you have to say for yourself?" Alistair asked him, not in the least affected by the fact he was still wearing his kitten pyjamas.

"I want a lawyer," the boy said as he glared back at him.

THE NEXT MORNING I slept in until nine. It had been a late night for all of us, especially Ivan, the boy who got arrested for stealing, since the jewellery he had been carrying was indeed stolen. They contained jewellery from both Put a Ring on It and the home invasion.

So far he was keeping silent about who his mates were, but I was certain it was only a matter of time.

I was about to go down to the bookshop when my doorbell rang. Christina was already downstairs, opening up the shop so I rushed down to get the door.

Emblyn stood in front of me with a worried look on her face. She looked over her shoulder.

"May I come in?"

"Of course. Don't you start work soon?" I asked as I stepped aside.

"Yeah, so I don't have much time."

I felt an uneasy feeling in the pit of my stomach. "What is it?" My voice was soft, as if I was afraid that speaking any louder would scare her off.

She was tugging on the sleeve of her jumper and avoided eye contact with me.

"Was it Elijah? Did he do something?"

"No, no," she said, but there was some hesitation, which made me think that it did have something to do with him.

"Okay," I said calmly and smiled at her to reassure her. "Do you want to go upstairs?"

"No. Look, I went on my date with Elijah last night and it was going great. But then he got a phone call and we had to go. I had to stay in the car but he drove me to the woods and was talking with someone he seemed to be afraid of. I couldn't see what they were doing. He disappeared behind the other guy's van and was out of sight. And then one of his other mates was caught in relation to the thefts."

"That bloke, Ivan, he's a friend of Elijah?"

Emblyn nodded. "I tried to ask him what's going on, but he told me it was safer if I stayed out of it. He just seemed really scared, Maggie. I want to help him, but I don't know what to do." Tears welled up in her eyes.

"Come here," I said and pulled her into a hug. "It's going to be okay."

I made sure that Emblyn was comfortable on my sofa and handed her Snowball to cuddle. Then I texted Nancy to ask her if she could do without Emblyn for an hour, which was fine. And then I phoned Alistair. He was there within ten minutes.

"Is she okay?" He asked as he stepped inside.

"Yeah, just a bit freaked out." I told him what she'd told me.

"You did the right thing, calling me."

"I know. Thank you for coming." I smiled.

"I'll always be here if you need me." He squeezed my arm.

"And I for you." I put my hand on his, then nodded to the stairs.

He followed me up to the flat and headed into the living room while I went to the kitchen to get them both tea. I was as curious as could be, but I had to restrain myself. Alistair was the right person for her to talk to and what kind of host would I be if I didn't provide tea at such a crucial time?

I returned and handed Emblyn her mug. She took it without looking at me. I put Alistair's on the coffee table. He was sitting on it so that he was directly facing Emblyn. He was scribbling in his notebook, neither of them currently talking.

I wasn't sure what to do. Did Emblyn want me here, or did she prefer being alone with Alistair? I decided to retreat to the kitchen and wait there. After seven biscuits—but who was counting? Nobody. So technically, I had zero—Alistair called me. Emblyn was in the corridor by the stairs.

"Thanks, Mags. I'm going to work now." She hugged me and gave an awkward wave to Alistair. Her footfalls were quick as she rushed down the steps. A moment later, the door shut. She'd used the door to the shop because it would be a faster way to Nancy's.

I turned to him and cleared my throat.

"You're dying of curiosity, aren't you?" He grinned.

"Maybe."

"Will you explode if I don't tell you?"

I chuckled. "No. I realise she may have asked you to keep it quiet, and I wouldn't want you to betray her trust."

A tender look displayed in his eyes. "Well, she didn't. Elijah went to meet someone in a van and she had gotten a phone call from someone registered in his phone as J. She also told me a bit more about his friends and some shady stuff that they've been into. Though Emblyn has never seen them do anything terribly wrong. The guy that Elijah met gave him a big envelope, which I'm guessing was money."

"Do you think it's related to what we witnessed yesterday?"

"Yes. But I have to prove it first."

"Let's get that proof then. Where are we going first?"

His eyebrow shot up. "I'm taking DC Daniels and maybe even a constable and we're going to pay Elijah and Johnny a visit. Earlier today I found a connection between Ivan and Johnny—they're family—and I think Johnny's got everything to do with this. First I need to hear Elijah's side."

"See, we're finally getting somewhere and now I'm missing all the action." I stuck out my bottom lip.

Alistair touched my chin. "Don't pout. This is a good thing. You stick to fictional crimes, and I'll worry about the real ones. I'll keep you updated, though." He brushed my chin with his thumb.

I lowered his hand so I could kiss him on the cheek.

His eyes widened. "What's that for?"

"For your help."

He leaned forward until our lips touched.

"What's that for?" I whispered.

"For being you."

Chapter Twenty-Nine

Peace and quiet returned to my flat after Alistair left, although my heart was still beating fast from the kiss. A girl could get used to those.

Detective Black was silently judging me from the corner of the living room. Probably because I was taking a moment to be distracted.

Right. Back to the new clues.

If Johnny was involving these kids in his drug dealing and with the robberies, then did it have to do with Valerie's murder? Was that the money she had been talking about? Was she planning on telling someone? Had she betrayed her husband in some way?

But how did they meet outside of the Pembroke if they hadn't phoned or texted? There had been nothing on her phone, which is why I always figured it was one of the actors. Someone who had told her in person to meet her in the garden at midnight.

David said she'd been trying to win him back, so she would have agreed to meet him. She got along with Geoff and Warren, it seemed, so she would have met them as well. I seriously doubted she would want to meet up with Brenda, unless she'd given an interesting reason.

Either way, I just didn't think it would have been Johnny.

"We know that she would manipulate in order to get what she wanted. I mean, she lied about being pregnant in order to get David to stay with her," Detective Black said.

"Yes."

"And she mentioned that she'd be getting more money. So she clearly had a plan of some sort."

"Maybe she meant Johnny when she said that. Perhaps she knew about the robberies."

Detective Black touched his moustache. "Could be possible."

"Why mention it, though? Was she boasting? Or did she want to use her money for something? Invest in the drama club?"

"What if she was looking to leave her husband? He didn't support her acting. It seemed like that was something she genuinely cared about."

I pursed my lips as I contemplated this. David had assumed she wanted to get back together with him because she couldn't stand being the one who was dumped, but what if her feelings for him were true and she wanted to be with him instead of Johnny? It would explain her desperation.

Yet, I didn't understand why she wanted to piss off Brenda so much by telling her the imaginary baby was Geoff's. Perhaps a visit to Warren would be a next good step. I wanted to know more about that particular fight between Valerie and Brenda.

WARREN LIVED IN A FLAT in Woolfield. It was a small building with grey bricks and French balconies. Warren worked from home on most days, so it hadn't been difficult to set up a quick meeting. I had brought Eddie along and had Brian cover for him at The Wicked Bookworm.

"And this is a guy who's been in the army, right?" Eddie asked after I rang the doorbell.

"Yes." I eyed him.

"Cool. Cool. Cool." He stretched his arms as if he was preparing for something.

"Relax. I'm sure he won't try to kill us."

He narrowed his eyes at me. "How sure?"

I pretended to think. "Fifty-five percent."

He started to sputter but then the door opened. This was the first time I saw him in his normal clothes and in this case he was wearing a tight black shirt and jeans. His muscles were hard to ignore and next to me Eddie made a squealing sound.

"Nice to see you again, Maggie," Warren said politely. "And you too, Eddie."

"Thanks for agreeing to meet with us." I smiled, hoping he wouldn't notice Eddie's increased nervousness.

His flat was tidy and minimalistic. The colours were mostly grey, black, and white. A Scandinavian police detective with a drinking problem would fit right in.

"Tea?" Warren asked as he started pouring himself a cup.

"No, thanks. We won't be long." I sat down on the sofa and Eddie followed suit.

"I understand you wanted to talk about Valerie. She was a good girl, but she just had a few issues."

"Especially with Brenda."

"Yes, but I don't think Brenda would have done anything to hurt her. I mean, she did hit her, but that was because Valerie had just told her she had gotten pregnant with her husband."

"Even though it was a lie," I said. "Why do you think she told Brenda that?"

Warren sighed and put his cup of tea on the side table before he plopped down in a leather armchair. "The only person she seemed to have a problem with was Brenda. They didn't like each other. Brenda wanted better roles, but Valerie was young and attractive and Geoff knew what would sell tickets. It was really that simple. My guess is that Valerie told that lie to break up Brenda and Geoff and get rid of her. She cared a lot about acting and a lot about the Dramateers."

"Why?"

Warren shrugged. "She didn't have anyone else and she loved being the centre of attention."

"That much was obvious," Eddie mumbled.

"I did see her have hushed conversations with Geoff, though." Warren frowned. "I'm sure it was nothing, but Geoff had looked upset and Valerie kind of...smug. I don't know why. I guessed it had something to do with Brenda, but I'm not sure."

"When did you see these hushed conversations?" I asked.

"A few weeks before that weekend. It was after the only fight I'd ever seen them have."

I perked up at this. "Valerie and Geoff?"

He nodded. "She had arranged a reporter to come and interview all of us. Geoff wasn't happy about that."

"Why not? Wouldn't that put all of you on the map?"

"Yes. It was going to be a big thing. It would be about all of us, The Dramateers, not just our acting journey but our lives as well. He was going to interview all of us and follow us around for a week. How Valerie had arranged it, I'm not sure."

Detective Black stood behind Warren. "There was probably a lot of flirting involved."

"Is that why she mentioned she'd be getting a lot of money soon?"

Warren raised his eyebrows. "I hadn't heard her talk about that, but it's possible she meant that. She had high hopes for the next show."

"Right. But then she died."

He blinked a few times and looked down at his hands. "She really was excited for that show. It's just too bad that she had such a crappy life before she died. That Johnny was bad news."

I nodded. "Very bad."

"Oh, I completely forgot to ask the police about this. But perhaps you could ask them for me."

"Ask what?"

"She had a key card from my gym. She used my locker at Get Fit for acting stuff that she didn't want about the house. I never use that locker anyway, but since she's...you know, I'd like it back."

Eddie and I exchanged a look. "She used your gym locker?"

"Yeah." He paused. "What?"

"I'M SORRY," ALISTAIR said. "We never found any gym key card on her. Not in her wallet, not anywhere."

"Do you think Johnny has it?"

"He's in custody now. I can check." We were at the police station where it was nice and quiet. We stood by a coffee machine while Alistair poured himself a cup.

"So, what's the scoop? What's going on?"

Alistair's jawline tensed and there was a hair at the back of his head which stood up straight. It was the equivalent of not wearing any shoes to work.

I had to fight the urge to run my hand over it.

"The good news is that Johnny is talking. He wants a reduced sentence for complying. He knows he's screwed."

"The bad news?" I asked.

"Well, I suppose it's not bad news, it's good that we know, but," he paused and gave me a certain look, "he's the one who tried to run you over." His eyes darkened.

Eddie gasped next to me.

"Oh."

"Is that all you have to say?" Eddie asked me. "Alistair, how illegal is it for me to go in there and punch him?"

Alistair gave Eddie a weary smile. "Trust me, I want to do the same thing, but Johnny's going to get what he deserves." He turned to me. "Are you okay?"

"Did he kill Valerie?"

"He says he didn't. He says that when you told him you were looking into the murder, he was afraid you'd find out about his illegal side hustle and when he saw you walking down the street, he saw an opportunity." He pressed his lips together and this time I recognised the look he gave me as scolding.

I looked down.

"So, what exactly was he doing?" Eddie asked.

"Ivan is Johnny's nephew. Him and Johnny aren't really good news. Ivan is friends with Elijah and two other boys. They kept daring each other to do stupid things, mostly involving damaging stuff. But then that soon escalated into breaking into places where people still lived and they started stealing. It became a dare to steal the most. At least, that's how Ivan presented it at first, but really, it was Johnny's idea. He worked jobs where those people got robbed, including at the jewellery store. He also had fake guns in his possession, which were used during the home invasion. Elijah wasn't there, luckily, but his other friends were."

"Wow," I said.

"Anyway, the other kids thought that Ivan returned the stolen stuff, because he said that he would. But they soon found out that wasn't the case, and when they wanted out, Johnny showed up with a gun to threaten them. They were afraid of Ivan and Johnny."

"Was he also planning to get them involved in the drugs?" I asked.

"He says not, so I'll guess we'll never know. Maybe theft was going to be Johnny's new interest." Alistair shrugged. A sign that he was tired. "Look, we'll go to the gym and get that locker opened. Whatever is in there, we'll find it."

"Okay. We'll get out of your hair," I said.

Alistair shot Eddie a look. I glanced back and forth between them.

"Err," Eddie said. "I'll be outside." He dashed off.

I looked at him expectantly.

"I'm sorry. I didn't mean to imply it was your fault that you nearly got run over. I'm just—I don't want you to get hurt."

I kissed him on his mouth. "I know."

He blushed and glanced around the police station.

I supposed it wasn't terribly professional to kiss at his place of work, but I couldn't help it. When he said things like that I wanted to kiss him. And why not do the things that made me happy?

Without looking back at him, I left the police station and joined Eddie outside.

"So what now?" he asked as rain started to fall.

"I have no clue," I said.

Chapter Thirty

It was the day before Halloween, which meant that I went pumpkin carving at Eleanor's with the women from the book club. Miles had announced he was going to throw a Halloween party at his mansion tomorrow for anyone who wanted to come, since he wanted to move on from the murder.

Alistair had opened the locker but nothing had been inside, which led me to believe that the killer may have gotten to it, but there were no cameras by the lockers and it was impossible to figure out who had entered. Still, Alistair had pulled an all-nighter with DC Daniels to see if they could spot any familiar faces entering the gym—apart from Warren—but nothing.

Of course, that meant that Warren was a suspect. He could have been lying about the key card, or he could have been telling the truth and perhaps he was the one that had killed her and then took whatever it was from his locker. Assuming that was the reason she had been killed.

So, still a lot of speculation. I didn't like that.

And yet I was in a good mood. Halloween was nearly here. Today we'd carve pumpkins and tonight I'd watch witchy and spooky films with Christina and Eddie. I had invited Alistair as well, but he wasn't sure if he would make it.

It was Friday and both Eddie and Christina were working, but I had managed to convince Miles to join us. Occasionally he had Friday afternoons off and today was no different.

I hadn't told the ladies yet. They'd probably be swooning all afternoon.

Miles met me halfway to the vicarage.

"Ready for some carving?" I asked him.

He wore an orange scarf and a long black coat. "I haven't done this since I was a kid, to be honest. Why do you guys do this exactly?"

"Because it's fun. We drink wine and gossip and try to make the most creative pumpkins."

"I see. Well, I'm eager to make this a tradition, then."

I gave a half-smile. "I promise you'll like it."

"I'm sure I will. The people here are beginning to grow on me. Sorry to hear that the murder investigation is at a stand still. Alistair informed me about the latest."

"Yeah, I know. It sucks." I couldn't wait any longer. "What will happen to the teenagers that Johnny and Ivan involved in their schemes?"

Miles glanced at me. "Three of them were underage, but Elijah is eighteen. Still, they were accomplices against their will and they were terrified. The ones that are really in trouble are Ivan and Johnny, especially Johnny."

"Good," I said.

I hadn't spoken to Emblyn much. She had taken days off from working at Nancy's and had been quiet. I could hardly blame her. She had come too close to something very dangerous.

"Despite the horrendous murder that took place, I've put up the website and the Pembroke is officially for hire. It also means that Geoff is coming round this afternoon because I want to hire him as my accountant."

"Really?"

Miles nodded. "I need someone and I figured, why not him?"

"I'm sure he'll be pleased, since he's interested in wealthy new clients."

"Oh, yes. I'm pretty sure he handed me his business card three times since the start of the murder mystery weekend."

It wasn't a bad idea for me to get an accountant as well, probably.

We arrived at the vicarage. Eleanor had decorated her home with fake candles that flickered in dark corners, self-made ghosts hanging from strings, fake skeletons, and weirdly coloured drinks that she'd put in lemonade pitchers. Harold had made a playlist of all kinds of Halloween-related music and it was playing softly in the background.

"Wow. I feel like I should have worn my Halloween costume," Miles said.

"I know. We only do that on Halloween itself, though. What are you going as tomorrow?"

He grinned at me. "You'll see."

"It's going to be something lame, isn't it?"

"No, it's not. What makes you think that?"

"Because you're too excited about it."

He folded his arms. "Mean."

Eleanor greeted us and directed us to get drinks and snacks first. She had set several tables in both her kitchen and living room with pumpkins and knives. Most of the women were here already, cackling animatedly. They dimmed down when they spotted the handsome specimen that was Miles and immediately wanted to show him their pumpkins.

AN HOUR LATER MILES went home to get ready for Geoff. He had carved four pumpkins and had made one that looked surprised, one that was throwing up its own guts, one that looked smug, and one that looked like a vampire.

I had managed to make one that resembled a Minion, one with square teeth, and a lady pumpkin with a kissy face.

Poppy was always surprisingly good at this. She had made a merry-go-round on a pumpkin once. And even made an Alice in Wonderland pumpkin. This year she carved out the silhouette of a werewolf and a mermaid.

Ava was the queen of inappropriate carvings. Last year she had carved two unicorns mating and a witch with a suspicious looking staff. This year she seemed to be good and was making murder-related pumpkins. Lots of weapons and only one pumpkin with a butt carving.

I was washing my hands in the kitchen, about to go for another round of snacks and a drink, when Callum entered through the kitchen. He was holding a bag which clinked, as if he had brought bottles.

"Hey, what are you doing here?"

"Just came to prepare a new batch of drinks. I offered to make spooky beverages today and I'll even do so tomorrow at Miles's Halloween party. He's so dreamy."

I chuckled. "That's awesome. The drinks taste so lovely. Much better than the wine that Olivia and Lily always bring. But don't tell them that."

"My lips are sealed, darling." He put down the bag on the counter. "Oh, by the way. You showed me that picture of that acting group, right? The Dramateers?"

My heartbeat sped up. "Yeah."

"I checked with a mate of mine, he knows *everyone* related to acting in any way on this side of the country. He recognised Geoff, said that there was this minor scandal and that he was suspected of embezzling. Never proven and it was done on a small scale, but there were rumours."

My mouth opened and then closed.

Gears were turning.

"Are you okay?" Callum asked. "You look like you swallowed a piece of Lego."

"I gotta go." I ran straight out of the kitchen and outside. As I ran all the way to the Pembroke without my coat on, I tried to dial Alistair's number. It took me three tries to actually ring him.

He didn't pick up, so I left a message.

I ran past Pandora who had jumped on top of a stroller, terrorising the young mother who tried to defend her baby with her umbrella.

I still didn't stop and arrived at the estate completely out of breath. Working out was definitely going to be on my to-do list in the near future. If only so I could get to killers quicker.

Without trying the front doors first, I went around the back and entered the kitchen. I listened, but everything was quiet. I was panting like a dog in labour and had to collect myself. Geoff and Miles would simply be chatting and I didn't want to alarm Geoff.

"They'll be in his study," Detective Black said. "And it may not be a bad idea to bring a weapon."

I glanced around the kitchen and picked my instrument of destruction. With a paper towel I dabbed my face and then I strode to the staircase and made my way up to Miles's office.

The door was ajar and I heard Geoff's voice. "Just stay down and let me think." He sounded panicked.

Oh, no.

"Whatever happened, looks like Miles is in trouble," Detective Black said.

I edged closer to the door and peered inside the room.

Miles was on the floor, blood dripping from his temple. He looked pale and held out his hand to Geoff who was holding a poker from the fireplace. Neither of them had spotted me.

I started dialling the number of the police station, so that I could be sure that someone was on their way, but at that moment Geoff looked at the door. His eyes widened and his nostrils flared.

"Okay, stay calm," Detective Black said. "Just do as he says and stall him."

"You there!" he shouted.

I held my phone behind my back, then opened the door and stepped inside.

Geoff advanced, knocked the rolling pin out of my hand, then roughly grabbed my arm, throwing me towards the desk where Miles was. He got up and held me to prevent me from tripping.

"Are you okay?" I whispered to Miles while Geoff checked the hall and then shut the door.

"I'm fine. Are you alright?"

I nodded. "I phoned Alistair. He didn't pick up but I left a message." My phone was still in my hand. "What happened?"

"I saw the gym card and realised he must have gotten whatever was in that locker. Which means he was involved in her murder. Or at least knew who the murderer was. Then I asked him about the gym and he attacked me."

"Stop whispering!" Geoff shouted. "Just shut up and let me think."

Great. He was contemplating whether or not it would be beneficial for him to murder us.

I pressed the recording button on my phone. Just in case his attack on Miles wasn't enough to put him behind bars.

"Was it you or her that decided to meet in the garden at midnight?" I asked, my voice steady and not too loud. I focussed on his collar because I was afraid that direct eye contact would agitate him even more.

"I—I did. I wanted her to leave me alone. I begged her even. And she laughed."

"She was blackmailing you and then *laughed* at you? She deserved to be taught a lesson," I said.

He ran his hand through his hair, still holding the poker in his other hand.

"She found out you were skimming money from your rich clients and wanted in, didn't she?"

"She wanted to help me get new clients and get a cut of the money. But then she decided to move to London, start over. And she wanted a big cut or she'd tell the police. I knew she was bluffing, I knew it. But she wouldn't let go."

"She was just as eager to be rich as you were."

"No, no. This was my plan. We deserve to be rich. She was just—she was just selfish. She was a user. She had a notebook where she kept track of any dirt or weaknesses she could find. And she hurt people when she didn't get what she wanted. She said that she'd break me and Brenda up if she had to. Then when I said nothing, she smirked and turned around and I just grabbed her. I had to."

I nodded. "Of course. She gave you no choice. She was going to destroy your life. It was her or you."

"Exactly. I had to do it. And I'm sorry, but I can't let you go." He started touching his breast pocket and took out a lighter. Then he moved towards the globe where Miles kept his liquor.

"Err, just one thing," I said, taking a statue of a panther from Miles's desk. I bridged the gap between us.

He looked up and I hit him with the statue. He fell against the wall and I quickly grabbed the poker from him while he groaned.

Miles swayed when he came over but he grabbed Geoff's ankles while I pushed his hands behind his back. My own hands were shaking and my legs felt like jelly.

The door was thrown open and Alistair and DC Daniels burst in the room with frantic expressions on their faces.

"Hello. Did you order a murderer?" I asked.

Chapter Thirty-One

Miles needed a few stitches, but at least Geoff readily confessed to killing Valerie. Valerie's notebook was more an account of the people in her life and important information about them and it was found in Brenda's possession. Geoff had been right that Valerie had been a user, but part of me also couldn't help but think that she was very lost and genuinely hurt when David broke up with her.

Brenda had known about the murder, even if Geoff hadn't initially known that she knew. Yeah, it gave me a headache too.

She eventually admitted to Geoff that she knew about the murder and after he had retrieved Valerie's notebook, she had promised to destroy it. The fact that she hadn't probably indicated that she didn't fully trust him and I suspect she was reading her way through it to find out if he had ever been unfaithful.

The notebook proved that Valerie knew about his past and the suspected embezzlement and she had started digging into his current work as an accountant. Just like with Johnny, he had made money illegally and she wanted to use that against him.

She also knew about the drugs, even though she had written that Johnny wasn't aware of that. In fact, he had worked hard to keep her out of it. At least that was something.

All of this meant that the murder of Valerie Cooke was finally closed and we could go back to normal. In this case, normal meant we were all dressed up as monsters, ready to have a good time.

Eleanor had made arrangements to help decorate the Pembroke's ground floor. There was music in every room and the kitchen was open to everyone as well. Snacks and drinks were around each corner and we had the opportunity to talk, dance, and snack. Miles had even created a game room with Twister, a dart board, and board games.

I was dressed as a Victorian woman and arrived with Christina, who was a fairy. The first people I spotted were Eddie, dressed as a zombie, and Nancy, a witch. They were chatting together in the sizeable living/dining room.

The rest of the book club women were there as well and they had scattered about the room. Phoebe and Jessica were with Poppy by the snacks on the dining room table; they were dressed as the three musketeers. Eleanor was chatting with Ava and Olivia. Eleanor was dressed as a nun, Ava as a mermaid with coconuts over her breasts, and Olivia was dressed as a croissant.

Lily was chatting Miles's ear off. She was dressed as Einstein while Miles wore a Phantom of the Opera costume. He grinned when he spotted me.

I gave him a little wave. It was all the encouragement he needed to break away from Lily. She was probably still trying to set him up with her daughter.

"Nice outfit," I said as he approached me.

"You look quite lovely yourself." He gave a little bow.

"How are you feeling?"

He looked around. "Pretty good. There are a lot of happy faces here, including mine."

"Even though it has stitches?"

"Even though it has stitches. Thanks for saving my life."

I shook my head. "Alistair would have shown up and saved the day otherwise."

"But he didn't. You showed up and you saved the day. In fact, I think you'll need to be my bodyguard instead of the other way around."

"Oh, no. No more murders. Although I must confess that I've enjoyed solving them." I bit my lip.

"Yes, I've noticed that. You're also quite good at it. People are at ease around you, they let their guard down and you pick up on the small things they reveal then."

I shrugged. "It's just—I don't know, I like reading people."

"Me too. Which is why I understand. I'm also a little obsessed with finding out the truth, even if my job sometimes entails fighting the truth. I don't get to choose who I represent. But when I get to represent someone innocent and I have to fight for them, it's the best feeling." His eyes twinkled as he spoke.

I kind of had that same feeling when I was trying to solve the murder. I couldn't bring back the victim, but I could still fight for them in some way. I wondered if there was a deeper reason for me wanting to fight for the voiceless.

It didn't matter.

I smiled at Miles. "I really love what you're doing with the Pembroke, and you should throw more parties like this. We need them."

"That sounds like a plan." He looked off to the side. "Oh, I should greet more guests. I'll see you around."

"See you." I decided to make my way to the snack table and see what was there, but I was intercepted by Detective Black...no, wait.

"Alistair?" I said, my mouth open.

"Hey. Do you know who I am?" he asked, his cheeks reddening.

"Yeah. You're Detective Black."

Detective Black huffed and puffed next to me. "He looks nothing like me. I look way more handsome than he does. And that moustache of his looks like a caterpillar."

Alistair's eyes lit up. "Yes! You don't describe him in great detail, but this is the image I had in my mind from the get go."

Strange sensations filled my chest and we stared at each other for what must have been like a minute. Neither of us looked away.

"I want to show you something cool," I said, and took his hand.

He blinked. "Okay."

I went into the corridor and he followed me up the stairs and to the library, away from the humdrum of people.

I pulled him inside the quiet room filled with tall bookcases and closed the door.

"What did you want to show me? Did you fill Miles's bookcases with your books?" He put his hands in his pockets and smiled at me.

"Yes, but that's not what I want to show you." I grabbed his collar and pulled him against me, our lips crashing into each other like the sea hits the shore. His arm went around my waist and mine over his shoulders. We held on tightly as we continued to kiss.

After a few moments we came up for air.

"You kissed me," he said, breathlessly.

"I did."

"What does this me—"

"I love you. That's all that matters, okay?"

He nodded, the expression in his eyes lascivious. "I love you, too." His mouth met mine again and pushed me up against the door. We made out for a long time. It would have lasted even longer if my stomach hadn't rumbled.

He pulled away and laughed.

"I need snacks," I said.

He brushed my lips with his thumb. "Then snacks you shall have, milady."

I took his arm and we went down stairs. As soon as we reached the bottom of the stairs, there was a scream and a recognisable flapping sound.

"Get this winged monstrosity away from here!" shouted someone. I think it was Miles.

"Pandora," we said simultaneously.

"Looks like I'm up." Alistair moved towards the sound of mayhem and evil clucking while I couldn't help but giggle.

Before I could find the snack table, though, a woman in a beautiful black gown and with a mask on stopped me in my tracks.

She looked at me for a moment, then removed her mask.

I felt every muscle in my body stiffen.

"Hi, Maggie," her soft voice said. It sounded different from what I remembered.

"Hello, Mother."

Did you love *Booked For Murder*? Then you should read *The Exciting Life of a Minor Character*[1] by Morgan W. Silver!

[2]

Claire is sick of being a Minor Character. She despises the fact that the most exciting thing that's happened to her in four long years has been answering a phone.

She wants her own story, she wants more lines, and most of all, she wants adventure. Even if that means killing her Main Character. Unfortunately, only the Author has the power to kill Characters, but Claire will not be deterred by logic and facts.

---

1. https://books2read.com/u/mKDAXE

2. https://books2read.com/u/mKDAXE

Then, even though it's not supposed to be possible, someone is murdered in Character Central. It causes a widespread panic worse than the time they had a lemon shortage. After all, only the Author should have the ability to kill a Character.

With the threat of multiple victims as well as Erasure for all Characters, Claire must team up with the Main Character she wants to bring down. If all else fails, she may even have to take it up with the Author.

Read more at www.authormw.com.

Also by Morgan W. Silver

Maggie's Murder Mysteries
Prelude to Poison
Poised to Quill
Booked For Murder

Monday Moody
The Chrono Unit

Standalone
The Exciting Life of a Minor Character

Watch for more at www.authormw.com.

www.ingramcontent.com/pod-product-compliance
Lightning Source LLC
LaVergne TN
LVHW010318200726

843507LV00010B/1278